Lilliane

The Waite Family Series
Book 4

Kathi S. Barton

This is a work of fiction. Names, characters, places, and incidents are products of the author's imagination or are used fictitiously and are not to be construed as real. Any resemblance to actual events, locations, organizations, or person, living or dead, is entirely coincidental.

World Castle Publishing, LLC
Pensacola, Florida

Copyright © Kathi S. Barton 2012

Print ISBN: 9781938961304

eBook ISBN: 9781938961311

First Edition World Castle Publishing, LLC September 10, 2012

http://www.worldcastlepublishing.com

Cover: Karen Fuller

Photos: Shutterstock

Editor: Brieanna Robertson

Chapter 1

"All right, children, today we're going to learn the letter K. I want everyone to think of a word that begins with the letter K. Tommy?"

The morning noise of the class was shattered by a loud pop. Then three more in rapid order. Lilliane knew the sound— gunfire.

Looking at her class of kindergarteners, she realized that they knew it too. Calm, she thought, she needed to be calm. Walking slowly to the door, she spoke to the children.

"Tommy? Tell me a word that starts with the letter K."

His eyes looked wide with fear. "Miss Waite…was that…are we…?"

She clicked the lock on the door before she answered. "Yes, Tommy, it was guns. Class, I want all of you to remain calm. Violet, shut the windows. Portia, you and Samuel move all the desks over to the door just like we practiced. All right?"

"Yes, Miss Waite." Both of them got up and started lifting the desks and piling them in front of the door Lilliane had just locked. Violet remained frozen in place.

Lilliane went to the little girl and knelt down in front of her. "Violet, honey, we need to work together. Go lock the windows like you know how."

Lilliane had been teaching children how to protect themselves in the classroom since the incident several years ago where two boys had gone to school and killed their classmates. Lilliane didn't want her students to be victims, neither in life nor the classroom. But this was only the second time they'd done this and this time was not a training activity. Two more shots and both she and Violet jumped.

Turning to the others now huddled in the empty middle of the room, she nodded to the bathroom. "Go inside the bathroom, all of you, and Violet and I will be—"

The bullet ripped through the door. Lilliane stood as a flash of pain touched her. Ignoring it, she rushed the children into the bathroom as two more bullets entered the room. Billy dropped to the floor, his little chest covered in blood.

"Run!" she screamed at the others. Turning to get Violet, she nearly wept with anger. The little girl lay on the floor with a pool of blood surrounding her head.

The door to the front of the room shattered open after another bullet took out the lock. The desk, tiny against the strength of the adults on the other side, slid across the room. The gun was the only thing she saw as she dropped to the floor while glass and bullets danced around the room and her.

"Fucking bitch thinks she can keep us out," a rough, young voice said. Lilliane knew for as long as she lived she'd never forget his voice or what he'd said.

Lilliane made her way across the floor and when she was behind the door she stood up and threw her body against it. The gun clanged to the floor. Not even considering that she'd never fired one before, she scooped it up and turned it on the two men standing there.

Pain shot into her chest as another bullet ripped into her. She aimed her weapon at them and pulled the trigger.

~~~

Massacre. That would be the only way to describe the scene that Captain Peter Shall came to at the Jefferson Elementary School on this Monday morning. He shook his head as he walked around the cruisers and medical teams. What was the world coming to, he thought with a shudder, when a family couldn't even send their kids to school without fear?

Officer Colton Jamison came toward him with grim look. Peter was sure whatever he had to tell him, he wasn't going to like it.

"What do we have? And please tell me that the gunmen have been caught." Civilians were milling around, ambulance workers, and firefighters as well. There was a news van just pulling up; yellow tape prevented anyone from moving into the large school.

"Not caught, dead. Both of them. No identification, but we're working on that. Seven dead including them. Teacher, a..." Colton glanced down at his notebook. "Lilliane Waite, kindergarten teacher, shot them both as near as we can tell."

Peter started to grin then thought about what Colton had said. "Is she dead too? Please tell me she's not."

"No. Wounded, but nothing fatal that I could tell. She took four shots, one in the arm, shoulder, and thigh. The fourth hit her in the head. Medic said she's lucky, shot just grazed her. She lost one and a little boy is in guarded condition. Life flighting him out now with the teach."

Peter watched as the helicopter took off. Another hovering just above it was ready to land. He saw movement out of the corner of his eye and groaned when the mayor and her entourage walked toward him. Peter didn't want to have to play nice right now. He nearly turned away to go anywhere else when the news crew started to follow the mayor.

"Mayor Wilson, Ms. Holcomb." Peter nodded to both women. "This isn't a good time for a photo shoot. I got dead kids here and they'll be bringing them out soon."

Peter had no clue if that was true or not, but it had the desired effect. The mayor stopped and looked back at the cameraman and held up her hand. Peter hadn't bought himself much time, but hopefully enough for him to get away.

"I need something, captain. The parents are screaming for answers. What do I tell them?"

Peter had a list a mile long to tell her, but he knew that he'd be committing employment suicide if he even mentioned one thing. He only shook his head and thought, Someday. Someday, you will regret asking me that.

"The suspected gunmen are dead and we have a yet undetermined accounting of all victims. We do know that several are dead and the exact count is hard to determine until we do a complete sweep of the building."

She looked at him. Peter had too many years under his belt to be worried if he was giving anything away on his face. She looked and looked, but Peter knew she was going to get nothing. He could, however, see her thoughts as if she were writing them on her forehead for him to read. She didn't believe him. And she knew he was bluffing about the counts. He didn't care so long as he didn't call him on it.

"All right, but when you know something I want to know it as well. You hear me, captain? I will be in the loop," she told him through gritted teeth. He wondered if she would have any back teeth left if she stayed in office much longer.

"Of course. When I know positive answers and information, you'll be told as well." He felt the grin at her look, but fought it. "I need to go inside. Excuse me."

Peter walked in front of the school and saw that, for all their security measures, it didn't do them a great deal of good. The front doors had been shot out. The small alcove was full of his men and he sent two of them to the sidewalk to try and keep the parents under control. Stepping into the open air offices he could see the first causality.

A nice-looking woman. "Olivia," her name badge claimed, had taken a bullet to the chest that had ended her life. The medic near her and a crying older woman covered Olivia up as he walked by.

The gunmen hadn't gotten to the other offices back in this part of the rooms. Two bullets took out a picture of the president and another, the water cooler. Showing his badge, Peter was let into the large part of the school by security personnel on duty.

"You been here all day?" he asked the man that had opened the door. The man looked pale, but it could have been for any number of reasons. His name tag said he was "Donald."

"No, sir. The mayor...Miss Wilson, she called the firm. Had me placed. Don't know what I can do, but here I'm placed." Donald grinned.

Peter grinned as well. Both at the man and his apparent distaste of the mayor Wilson.

"Well, Donald, I'd like to keep my crime scene clear. Why don't you go on outside the yellow tape and wait for one of my men. I'll make sure your firm knows it was me that removed you."

Donald nodded then turned to leave. He stopped before going through he door. "Those kids...how many did them bastards get?"

Peter looked at the medical team coming toward him with a small body bag on the gurney he was pushing. "Too many, too damned many."

It was nearly six hours later that Peter stood in front of the camera. No one was happy with the news. The mayor had made him be the one to tell the world that a total of seven people had died, two of which were the suspected gunmen, one adult female, and four children.

Chapter 2

"All right, Margo. Let's try this again. Take a deep breath and hold it. When I tell you to push, we'll have that little fellow born." Cain loved this part at being a doctor, bringing new life into the world. Babies are what humanize us, he thought. Of course, he thought with a grin, they also make us worry warts. His personal cell phone vibrated in his pocket.

"I'm tired, Dr. Waite. Can't you just make him hold off for an hour or so until I can take a nap? I'll be better then." Cain glanced up at Margo's boyfriend when Margo whined again.

There was no way these two would last, he thought, and was glad they'd decided to give the baby up for adoption. Two sixteen-year-old kids had no right having children of their own. No matter what Cain thought of the ending process.

When his phone vibrated again, the reminder he'd missed a call, he was glad he'd tagged his message to call Alyssa, his wife, if there was an emergency. The only people who had this number were his sisters and their husbands and, of course, his wife.

"Come on, Margo. The sooner you listen and do what I need, the sooner we can get you to your nap. Come on now. Bear down like I told you."

It took another hour for the baby to make his appearance. Margo and the boyfriend—Cain had no clue what his name was as the kid had never made it to any of the appointments—were settled in her room nearly an hour after that. Cain was exhausted himself and looking forward to going home to his new baby boy, Connor, and Alyssa. Then he wanted to crawl into bed and sleep for several days. He was surprised when he saw her sitting in the waiting room. Then concerned when he saw her face.

Something had happened, he was sure of it. He started toward her when he noticed Damon Grant and Drew, his brother-in-law, with her.

"Alyssa? What's happened? Oh God, my mother again." Cain hoped that was all it was, but somehow, knew it wasn't.

"Cain, listen to me. Everyone is all right. Damon needs you to brief him on your patients that need you right now. Then we need to go to Nashville. Lilliane…there was a school shooting and she's been shot."

The room swam around him. Had it not been for Drew and Damon, he might well have fallen. Before he knew it, Cain was sitting in a plastic chair and his head was pushed between his knees.

"Stay with me, young man," Damon growled from above him. "Your family needs you."

Cain looked up at his wife who was kneeling in front of him. She smiled and Cain felt some of the weight lift off his chest.

"Lilliane is in surgery. She is expected to make a full recovery. She was shot four times. The bullet to her head was just a minor abrasion, but it still needed stitches, they said. Our plane is on the tarmac and your sisters have been picked up and are en route to there. Grace Anne is being picked up as well, and your sister Sin is being notified by her CO. She and Payton will be here too. How did the delivery go?"

The change in subject startled him. But he knew what she was doing. She was trying to help him absorb. He loved her all the more for it.

"Baby boy, seven pounds, ten ounces. Healthy and with his adoptive parents. What aren't you telling me?" he asked her with a smile.

"You always were too smart for your own good." She stood up when he did. "Your mother has been booked on a commercial flight, paid for with limo service to and from the hospital. And before you ask, yes, she's in a different hotel and not happy with me."

"Damned cheerful about that too, aren't you?" Cain looked at Drew as he spoke. "All I'm saying is your mom is a…peach. A nasty one with a huge pit."

Alyssa laughed. "He's not happy with me either. I made Drew call her. She wanted us to fly commercial and her to take the jet. He told her that it doesn't work that way."

Cain smiled. He'd bet his last buck more was said then that but didn't comment. Guinevere Waite hated Alyssa and vice versa. Alyssa would and could gladly never speak to his mother again, but kept a majorly civil tongue in her head when Cain had to go and see her.

Cain found himself in a bear hug and all the wind knocked out of his body. Damon Grant, for a man his age, could hug like a fullback in a game. Cain loved the man with all his heart.

After giving Damon a run down on his patients Cain, Drew, and Alyssa got going to the limo. Alyssa's phone rang as they were pulling away from the curb. Cain turned to Drew.

"What's she missing?" His wife was the richest woman in the world and according to the prenup he'd signed when they married, he was the richest man. What was hers, she'd said was his. No dividing of things, no splitting of property. If he wanted a divorce, he might as well kiss any future children goodbye because she was taking his nuts as her part of the divorce. And he believed her. That part wasn't written down, of course, but he believed her all the same.

Drew smiled before answering. "Dinner with the mayor, a fundraiser dinner where she was the guest speaker, and a luncheon at the Women's Of America club, none of which she wanted to attend anyway. Oh, and she left her brother in charge to go to the first two."

Alyssa's brother Nathan had been helping her out for the past several months since their mother had been murdered. Her other brother, Robert, had killed Shannon and had tried to kill Quinn and Drew's mother. It had been a nightmare since trying to sort out the different things they'd all been involved in since that day.

Within minutes of getting settled in their seats on the jet, they were gliding down the runway. One of the many things having money could provide, he supposed. Not that they were the idle rich. Both of them worked very hard and gave back so much.

Alyssa ran a huge corporation and not by sitting behind a desk. She attended board meetings, walked production lines, and knew every part of the company from top to bottom. He'd even helped her work a line or two at the different plants she ran when they were short staffed. She also got along with every member of management she employed and worked the kitchen line twice a week in the homeless shelters around the city. She also taught a class once a week on how to manage a business that some of the homeless attended.

In addition to the four homeless shelters around and about the city, she also managed two daycares centers, a clinic, trade school, and a hotel that no one but the homeless people ran and kept up. It had been rated one of the top five places to stay in the Zanesville area. Cain was very proud of his wife.

Not that he was a slug himself. He had his own practice, he volunteered twice weekly at the clinic, and he sat on a number of committees. When she got off the phone, she unbuckled and moved over to his lap.

"That was the police captain. A Peter Shall. He said that Lilliane is still in surgery but should be out when we land." Cain closed his eyes against the pain in his heart. "He said she was a hero. I assured him we knew that. He told me that she killed those gunmen with their own gun. Peter said that the two gunmen had enough ammo on them to kill each child and adult in that building and, according to what they'd found out, that was their intent."

Cain knew there was more, lots more, but Alyssa was giving it to him just the way she ran a board meeting. Details enough to remember then more as the person gathered facts. He didn't like it much, but knew to rush her wouldn't get him anywhere. Quinn held two of her triplets to her breast while she cried softly and Jazzie just sat still in her chair. Drew reached over, took his sister's hand, and held his wife, Quinn, to him as she cried. It wasn't until Cain's own son stirred that Alyssa got up to see to him.

He went to stand over her when she sat in a rocker that had been added to the plane in the last few months. She was nursing Connor. Connor Cain Waite, his little boy.

"I love you. I don't tell you that often enough, but I do. And I love you more with each passing day."

"I love you too, Cain." She snuggled Connor closer to her as she whispered the rest of the grim tale to him. "She lost two of her own. That little girl she loved, Violet, and a little boy who died at the hospital, Billy. She won't take that well when she finds out, if she doesn't know already."

Cain nodded. Lilliane had the tenderest heart he knew. He also knew his sister well enough to know that even though those men had tried to kill her and some of her own children, she would not have wanted to kill them. She would hate knowing that she caused their deaths.

The trip was uneventful and they landed an hour later. A limo waited for them and before they could move to the hospital Cain's phone vibrated again. It was Damon.

"Called in a favor for you down there. Lilliane, of course, is getting the best care and she is going to be fine. They removed the bullets without any muscle or bone damage. The graze to her left temple is nothing that they are concerned about. She'll have a hell of a headache, nothing else. The bullet in her thigh was deep, but missed the artery and because she was so athletic she'll not have any damage there either. They're putting her in a private wing so you all can stay with her. She'll be coming around about dinnertime."

Cain couldn't speak. He was so overwhelmed at that moment. Damon seemed to understand and said nothing. Alyssa took his hand and squeezed it. He returned it.

"Thank you," Cain managed after a bit. "Thank you so very much. I'll call you tonight."

Cain told his family and each of them seemed to take a deep breath. Lilliane was going to be all right.

Chapter 3

Shamus McKee looked at the mayhem that was normal in a large office, especially a large police station. He watched the man he'd been assigned to shadow and decided that he liked him. He found himself even admiring the man. Shamus looked at the board that seemed to be the focal point of the room and studied the pictures.

He tried to avoid looking at the two pictures of the dead children with their smiling school pictures along side of them. Even the pretty girl Olivia Bright had a gruesome picture alongside one that had been taken by the school she'd worked for until this morning. He concentrated on the map, the interior shot of the school.

He couldn't quite get what made him keep looking at it, but instinct told him there was something there. He looked over at Peter when he sat next to him.

"Hell of a way to start the day, isn't it? School shooting and not anything to go on other than a van rented to a man who's been dead for over ten years. And I have a bunch of dead folks and I can't tell anyone why they were killed. Sucks all the way around." Shamus didn't think he was required to answer, so he didn't.

"You find the names on the two who did this? I didn't think it'd be too hard with their prints." Shamus looked at the map again and felt the first touch of what it might be, but he turned away again. He knew if he forced it, it would never come.

"Nah, not yet. CODIS takes awhile. It's not like they show you on television, is it—an hour to solve a case?"

Combined DNA Index System or CODIS wasn't slow so much as overwhelmed. There could be as many in the system as there were snowflakes, Shamus thought. The criminal justice DNA database worked with all agencies to help make sure that all criminals were put behind bars and to make it a bit easier to get them there. The National DNA Index System or NDIS was considered one part of CODIS, the national level, containing the DNA profiles contributed by federal, state, and local participating forensic laboratories.

They both looked up when one of the officers came in with a hit on the prints.

Marc and Jimmy Chambers, brothers, had a very long list of priors. Nothing like what they had pulled this morning, but they did have a few things on their list to land them a few months stay in prison. Breaking and entering and assault with a weapon just to name a couple of them. Shamus looked at the pictures and thought they might have been doing a lot more hard stuff but hadn't been caught until today.

This time when Shamus glanced at the map on the wall, he had it. "The teacher that was shot, she or one of her students was the target. The Chambers, they went there specifically."

Pete looked at the wall and frowned. "How did you come up with that? I mean, I'm not saying you're wrong, but how did you come to that?"

Shamus walked up beside him and pointed to the hallway. "They took out only what they wanted from the office. People who might have been in their way. Sure they were going to kill them all, the amount of ammo they had would explain that, but look where the Waite woman's room is. They had to pass three other rooms, rooms that had just as many children in them as hers. They even passed another kindergarten class."

"But why?"

Shamus shrugged. "Could be she was seeing one of them. Could be that she owed them some money and they decided to come and make her pay. Don't know. There are a lot of sick people out there." Shamus looked at the picture of the pretty teacher. "Could be nothing at all."

When the information on the two killers was found it reinforced that someone was a target in the school. The men had had a great deal of money, just over ten grand, put into their account ten days before. The money had come in the form of a Western Union transfer.

Shamus and Peter went with the team that was going to their home to see what they could find. Shamus thought he was right, but he didn't have a good feeling about the why.

The woman was just too…well, wholesome for this. He thought she looked like someone who would be the girl next door and sex on a stick too. Her bright blue eyes and dark short hair had made him think of back porch swings and lemonade, a stupid thought for a man like him, but it was there all the same. But it was the look in her eyes that had him wanting to find her and a nice dark corner. And for whatever reason, it really pissed him off.

The house proved that Shamus was right. There were perhaps fifty pictures of the woman in various places around town. There were some close up and quite a few of them at the school. There was a hanging map of the school as well as a list of names that they would see when they went in. Christ, there was even a picture of the students in her classroom. But the telling thing was the large knife that stuck in the picture of the woman hanging next to a copy of their deposit slip for the ten grand.

It was near midnight before they left the house and they were no closer to finding the why than they had been before they got there. Shamus was in the front seat of the unmarked car when Peter told him that he was going to see the woman in the morning and asked if he would like to come along.

"Sure. I'd like to ask her a few questions of my own, one of which is why was she teaching the kids how to block the room with desks. Did she have an idea what was going down?"

~~~

Lilliane hurt. She hurt everywhere and wasn't afraid to say so with moans and tears. Opening her eyes was too much effort, but someone was prying them open for her and then had the nerve to flash a bright light into them.

"No" was about all she could manage before she realized her throat hurt and was as dry as the Sahara. She couldn't turn over either.

"Come on, Lilly Pad, open up. How else are you gonna be able to see how stupid Cain's hair looks?"

"Jazzie?" That couldn't be right. Why was Jazzie in her bedroom? She lived in Ohio with… "Cain?"

"Yes, baby, it's us. And for the record, my hair does not look stupid. I slept on it funny, that's all. Wake up, love, you're scaring Connor. Please?"

Lilliane tried to open her eyes, but the best she could manage was one. The other seemed to be covered up. She started to move it, but her arm seemed to not be working either.

"Can't see. Hurt. Happen?" Her mind was fuzzy and there seemed to be huge dark spots in her thoughts.

"Hello, Miss Waite. My name is Doctor Samson. Do you know where you are?"

Lilliane didn't know him either. But her head suddenly hurt. Pain, incredible pain, made her cry out and then there was nothing.

The next time she opened her eyes the room was bright. She still hurt, but not the pounding head like the other time. Slowly, she moved her head around to take in the room.

Hospital. She couldn't quite remember why she was there, only that she had been hurt. Frowning, she tried to think, but it hurt again so she let it go. There were a number of flowers around the room, bouquets of every color and style, but nothing much else. She moved her head to the right more and saw Alyssa and Sin. Tears formed in her eyes at the sight of the two of them holding babies. Clearing her throat she saw them look at her.

"Well hello, sleepyhead. How you feeling today?" Sin put the baby in her arms over her shoulder and walked toward her. "You need anything, pain meds, or something to drink?"

Lilliane was always surprised when she saw Sin. They were identical twins and when they were together, Lilliane couldn't help but be in awe at looking at a mirrored image of herself.

"Dry. Hurt but not bad. Is that Tonya?" She tried to focus on the baby, but it was just too difficult. Instead, she lay back on the bed and closed her eyes. "I can't remember what happened except that I got hurt."

The silence made her open her eyes again and look at the women. She didn't like the look they were giving her. She started to ask when Alyssa spoke up.

"The doctor said to let you remember on your own. I think it's a crock of shit, but hey, I'm just the sister here. I think you should be told and just get it over with."

Lilliane looked at Sin. "Tell me. You know you want to as well. Tell me what happened."

"What do you remember? Anything?" Sin laid the baby on the bed next to her and Sin took her hand. "Start with the beginning of what you remember."

She tried to think, but all she got was a pain in her head. "I don't know. It hurts to think about it."

She looked at the door again when someone came in. She didn't know either man and apparently neither did her sisters. When the men asked the other women to step out, of course both of them refused. Lilliane had to smile. She didn't think they'd do it either.

"We need to ask Miss Waite a few questions concerning the—"

"She doesn't remember anything. And you will so not tell her like this," Sin snapped at both men. "You'll come back when she's ready and not one second before or I'll let your commander know what a piece of dipshit he has in his employment."

The younger man laughed. "Army or special forces? Gotta be one or the other to think that you can just order around anyone you please. I'm thinking SF."

Sin flushed. "Special. And why? You think you got me pegged, soldier? I eat men like you for breakfast."

"Nope, just making an observation. We can come back when Miss Waite is up to it. We're not the bad guys here, just so you know. Miss Waite."

Lilliane stopped them before they left. "Stop. I want to…Sin, sit down and shut up. Or better yet, Alyssa, take her to the cafeteria and get her something sweet. I'm sure it'll turn sour before it gets past her lips, but there isn't any help for it." She pointed to the now vacant chairs. "Sit down and tell me."

The man laughed again. "You and your twin are bossy little things, aren't you? We don't want to go against doctor's orders. We can come back—"

"No. Now. And wouldn't it be better all around if you know what our names are? I'm Lilliane Waite; these are my sisters Sydney Cooperider and Alyssa Waite. Alyssa is married to my brother Cain and Sin is married to another cop, Payton. You are…"

"I'm Peter Shall. I spoke with you, Mrs. Waite, the other day, and this is my partner Shamus McKee. He's here on special assignment from his own department." Peter sat down. "There's been a shooting. What do you remember about it?"

Lilliane looked at the other man before she answered. "Special assignment for whatever happened or just in general?"

"General. You know the extent of your injuries, Miss. Waite? The reason I'm asking is because if you can remember what those are from, or at least what they look like, it may trigger your memory."

His voice was soft and kind, but the look in his eye made her think she was in trouble. But she did look down at the bandages on her body. Her thigh was injured, but she couldn't really see what had happened so she tossed the cover back. There was a thick padding there that had a bit of blood on it. Nothing came to mind.

Her head was bandaged as well and she knew that it wasn't severe or she'd be in more pain. Thinking hurt, but she thought maybe it was more because whatever had happened had been very bad. She looked at her arm.

"I've been shot, haven't I? Something…a gun. There was a gun and something about…they, there were two of them. They called me a bitch and told me that I couldn't get away."

The man nodded. "Yes. What else? Take your time. What about the two men? Did you see them?"

Did she? "I don't think so. The one shot into where I was…he… Oh my God, the children. He killed the…Sin."

Sin was suddenly there. "I'm sorry, baby. I'm right here. Shhhh. I've got you. This nice prick is going to leave the room now or I'm going to blow his nuts off."

Lilliane laughed. Sin had a way with words and the fact that she never raised her voice made it all the scarier.

Lilliane shook her head. "I love you very much, but this has to be done." She looked at the man sitting. "We heard the guns going off and they…Billy was shot first. The poor little thing, he was still breathing when… Violet and I were shot next. She was…I think she was in shock. When I turned around, she was gone." Tears streamed down her face at the thought of the little girl dead. "Violet took one to the head. She was gone before…before they forced the door. Billy's dead, isn't he?"

"Yes, ma'am. They did everything they could for him, but the bullet hit a part of his heart. He died in flight," the man called Peter said. "What do you remember about the men? Anything could be helpful."

She closed her eyes and used the skill she'd developed to remember the kids' names in her class. "Tall, both of them were tall. No accent or…they were white men. One of them had facial hair. I could see it peeking out from under the black knitted hat. Light-colored, brown maybe, or tan-colored. He wore a dark blue hooded jacket, I think…maybe it said 'Trojan' or something. Khaki pants, also a dark blue. Boots that was clean, very clean actually. The shorter man also had a knitted hat on. His was one like the hunters wear—the bright orange ones. A navy blue sweatshirt. Hummm, I think it was turned inside out. Also, he had on khaki pants, but his were the camouflage kind, greens and browns. They had a gun each. The one…the one that I picked up and used was heavy and shiny." She looked at Shamus. "Sin could tell you what kind, but I'm not as proficient as she or even you would be when it comes to weaponry."

Both men stared at her before Shamus laughed. "Impressive. I thought you didn't see them. That's perfect."

Lilliane flushed. "You asked me. I just wanted to help any way I could."

Sin stood up then and took a step toward Shamus. Lilliane might have stopped her, but Payton and her mother, Guinevere Waite, walked in. Lilliane couldn't help the groan that escaped. She hoped that her mother didn't hear it, but when Guinevere spoke, Lilliane knew that she had.

"I don't know what you have to groan about, young lady. You have managed to bring us all here for very little wrong with you. And she—" Guinevere pointed at Alyssa. "She made me take a commercial flight rather than let me sully her nice plane."

Chapter 4

Shamus looked at the older woman to see if she was joking. He'd been briefed on the family connections with the Howards and also that one of the sisters had married well. The Millers were a very wealthy family, as well as the Cooperiders. Shamus looked back at Lilliane and then at Sin and wondered if two women could look so much alike and be so different in temperament. Sin looked ready to explode while Lilliane looked like she wanted to crawl in a hole.

"Mrs. Waite, I take it?" Shamus stepped in front of Sin before blood was shed. "I'm Detective McKee. I'm still asking Miss Waite some questions and I was wondering if you wouldn't mind stepping back out into the hall."

"Yes, I do mind. She's my daughter no matter how much of a disappointment she is to me. Now get out of my way. I have a few things—"

"Why you fucking—"

Payton put his arm around his wife's waist and pulled her back. Shamus might have laughed, but she looked ready to do serious harm to the older woman. He cleared his throat and tried to calm the situation down without bursting out laughing.

"Mrs. Waite, if you can't offer any constructive help then I will have you removed." Shamus held up his hand and when she opened her mouth. "If the next words out of your mouth aren't, 'sure, Shamus, I'll wait in the hall,' then you can bet I'll call in the nice cop in the hall and have you removed."

He heard a laugh and glanced over at Alyssa to see her shove a blanket in her mouth. When a similar sound came from behind him he didn't even bother turning because he knew it was Sin, who was not trying to hide the sound.

"I'll have your badge for this. See if I don't make a few calls...why, my daughter-in-law over there is the richest woman in the world, though she never shares it. I'll have her call in a few favors and see—"

"I have to agree, Shamus. I'm sorry, but you'll have to call in the nice policeman to have her removed. And for the record, Guinevere, I would help anyone if it would get you away from me." Alyssa stood up and laid her son in the small seat on the floor. "Get out or so help me I'll help him throw you out."

The woman looked like she might have said more, but she simply glared at them all, turned on her heel, and left. When the door closed, the temperament of the room seemed to lighten. He felt someone pat him on the back and turned to look at Payton.

"Nicely done. I think I like you. Payton Cooperider. This spitfire is my wife, Sin. Thanks for not letting her kill her mom. It was a bit touchy there for a minute."

Peter let out a long breath. "I'll say. Shamus, I'm going to call into the department and see what else they've found. I'll be right back." He nodded once and left.

Shamus looked at the others in the room and waited to see if he was going to catch hell from the rest of them. When it was apparent they weren't but were seemingly packing up to leave, he looked over at Lilliane. "I can come back. I'm sorry about this, Miss. Waite." He started toward the door to find Peter. "I'll make sure that your mom is taken care of and tell her I'm sorry."

"Don't do that. She'll think she can come back in here. I don't think I can take her tonight. And it's Lilliane." She laid her head back on the bed as the others moved to give her a kiss and hug. "I can't leave like the rest of them can."

"Don't. She'll need to finish this and we're going to feed the babies. You stay until she throws you out." Alyssa stuck out her hand. "I'm very glad to meet you, Shamus. I'd like for you to come to the hotel later and meet my husband. He'll have some questions for you, I'm sure."

"All right. Peter and I can do that." Shamus couldn't think what she thought he could tell them that they probably didn't already know, but he wanted to meet the brother. When they were alone, he looked over at Lilliane.

"They really don't have to feed the babies. Connor just ate and Tonya takes a bottle, which I'm sure Sin had with her. They just want to make sure my mother doesn't come back. She really isn't a nice person." Lilliane straightened the blanket with her good hand. "She never liked any of us."

Shamus walked toward the bed and helped her make the covers lay flat. He was amazed at how tiny she looked all bandaged up like she was. He sat in the chair when she seemed satisfied with the bed.

"My mother passed away when I was a baby. I never knew her. My father loved her so much that he died soon after I got out of school, to be with her he told me. I joined the Army right out of high school to try and find the family they said that I would have. All I found was a disciplined way of life that I enjoyed." He grinned at her. "I'm not sure why I told you that. I don't think I've ever told anyone that before."

"I'm a good listener. That's why I made a good teacher. I loved to listen to the children and see what they needed and once I found it, it was a piece of cake to teach them." She reached for the water and he stood to give it to her. When she pulled away from the straw she thanked him.

Shamus sat on the edge of the bed and looked at her. "You're very beautiful. If I had a teacher like you I would have paid more attention to my lessons. Or maybe not. Did your kids have crushes on you?"

"No, yes, I suppose. There was always one or two who would give me those soulful eyes and puppy dog looks. I wasn't as immune to them as you'd think. I love…loved teaching."

"Loved? You're not going to stop teaching, are you? You can't do that, you know. You have to get back up on the horse, as they say, and keep riding." He pushed the hair from her cheek and thought about how soft it was. "Teachers are our first line of defense in making sure we have better children."

His voice had gotten husky and he wondered if she noticed. He wanted to touch her more, but didn't want to frighten her. When she licked her lips Shamus leaned forward slowly, wondering if kissing her would be a wise idea.

"I don't think I can face a classroom…are you going to kiss me, detective?" Her voice had lowered as well and, when she licked her lips again, he groaned.

"I would love to. Is that an invitation, Miss Lilliane? Because the thought of tasting your mouth is all I can think about right now." He brushed his mouth over hers slowly. "Can I have your mouth, a taste of you?"

Her answer was to lean forward and press hers lips over his. The contact was brief, but it was all the permission he needed. Cupping the back of her head he brought her to him and kissed her. When she opened her mouth under his Shamus shifted on the bed and brought her closer as gently as he could.

Ambrosia. Heaven. Heat. Shamus had never tasted anything more lethal or more desirable in his entire life. When he touched his tongue to hers, she moaned deeply and put her hand on his chest. Shamus was sure that she could feel his heart pounding and wanted to press her back against the bed and touch her everywhere. But a knock at the door had him pulling away. When she whimpered he nearly snarled at whoever was there to get the hell out so he could do just what he wanted. Instead, he kissed her again and stood.

"There's someone at the door. Do I let them in or do you need a moment or two? I need a few hours, but I doubt that they're here to see me."

She blushed prettily at him and then dropped her head. "I'm not sure what came over me. I don't kiss people…I never kiss strangers. No matter how good-looking…you know, just tell them to go away on your way out, please. I'm…I have a headache and I'm tired."

Shamus leaned down and kissed her again. Not as hard and certainly not as much as he wanted to, but he needed to touch her. He lifted her chin. "I kissed you, not the other way around. Though I have to admit, I certainly enjoyed it when you kissed me back. And just for the record, I'd like to do it again. Actually, I'd like to do a lot more than just kiss you." He stood up when the knock came again. "But for now I'll let the person in and hang around outside to wait on my partner."

He went to the door and turned the knob only to find it locked. He looked at her and smiled. Someone had locked them in. He wondered who he had to thank for that and decided it was her twin. He blew Lilliane a kiss and opened the door to the nurse.

"That door isn't to be locked. What if there had been an emergency?" she snapped at him as they stood just inside the doorway.

"I'm sorry. I was asking Miss Waite some questions about the shooting at the school and I didn't want her mother to come in and interrupt us. She can be a bit…caustic, if you know what I mean."

The nurse, Sasha Jo Johnson, her name tag read, snorted and continued in hushed tones. "Yeah, she's a real piece of work that one is. I think if someone was real smart they'd tape her mouth closed then ship her off to another planet. She's been harassing my nurses for over an hour trying to get them to give her something for pain. Something to knock her out, she said. I wanted to tell her that I'd do that for free, but I don't think she'd like the results." They both looked over at Lilliane when she laughed. "I almost feel sorry for you, miss, having that for a mother."

"You've no idea. I moved here when I turned eighteen when my sister Sin left for the service. It was that or kill myself. I found teaching a whole lot...oh my God. I can't believe I said that."

Shamus went back to the bed and held her. When he turned around, the nurse was gone and he'd bet his last buck that the door was locked again. He held Lilliane until she stopped crying and then held her a bit longer. When she was still for a few minutes, he realized she was asleep and laid her gently on the bed. With a quick kiss to her forehead, he left the room. And sure enough, the door was locked.

~~~

Sin waited for Shamus to come out of the room. She liked the man, but wanted to make sure before he got her full approval. She stepped in front of him when he started down the hall. He didn't jump like she'd expected him to, but simply smiled at her. "You're very quiet on your feet, Mrs. Cooperider. I can see that you did well in the special services. What can I do for you?"

"You stood up to our mother, why?" she asked as the lead him toward the stairs. "Most people who just meet her seem to back off."

"But not you and especially not for your sister. Where are you taking me? I assure you there are people who know where I am."

His grin was charming, but she still didn't have all her answers. "I'm taking you to the cafeteria. My family wants to talk to you. Your partner is already aware of me coming to get you." She knew she didn't have much time so she cut to the heart of the matter. "What do you plan on doing about the attraction with my sister?"

He stopped on the stair and stared at her before he continued on. "You simply say what you think, don't you? All right, my intentions are none of your business. That blunt enough for you? She's a witness in a horrific crime."

"You're not going to tell me that that's all she is to you because I won't believe it. The sparks were coming off you and her like the fourth of July. And just so you know, I'm not the only one who noticed. My sister Alyssa noticed it as well and she's not all that observant, if you ask me."

"But I didn't." They came to the bottom of the flight of stairs and he stopped to look at her. She liked it when someone looked her in the eye; it made her feel like they might tell her the truth. "You tell me something and I might be inclined to tell you something. Deal?"

She didn't usually make deals that involved her family, but she was really beginning to like this man. "Okay, deal. But if you give me shit, I'll hunt you down. Lilliane didn't just move away to become a teacher in rural America. She moved to hide from our parents. Mother and Father treated her like their personal slave and she took it. I'd like to see her hooked up with someone who can stand up for her or with her. But I don't know if that's you or not."

"Fair enough, but I'm not sure it's me either. I like her and I'd like to get to know her better, but... What I'm going to tell you is strictly between the two of us. I don't want to—"

"I don't keep secrets from my husband. You tell me, you are telling him as well." Sin stuck out her hand. "But he can keep a secret too."

He took her hand and didn't give her a girly handshake like most men did. "All right. I think your sister was the target in this shooting. Not only was she the target, but I fear they'll try again. She either knows something or they think she does."

"What kind of something? If you think Lilliane is involved in anything illegal then you couldn't be more off the mark." He was shaking his head before she finished. "Then what could it be?"

"I don't know. Before I came here today, I thought she looked too wholesome to be involved in the shooting. Now…well, now I know she isn't. But someone is. Who do you know that would want to take her out? Do you know of enemies? Anyone who would have a grudge against her?"

Sin started to say hell no, but thought first. She'd been away for too long to know that answer for certainty. She looked at the door they'd yet to go through. She needed more information before she could answer that. For one, why did he think she was the target?

"I've been gone for a long time so I couldn't say. I've lost touch with my family over the years and it hasn't been until the death of my father and also me getting injured in the service that I've been home. Less than a year I guess." Sin looked at Shamus again. "But I can find out. My family is going to try and convince her to come back to Ohio with us."

Shamus nodded and made Sin realize that he knew something more than she did. Before she could ask, he told her. "She wants to give up teaching. She said she doesn't think she can face a classroom again. I don't think that's a good idea. Also, she said she had to move from your parents or kill herself. Was it that bad?"

"For her, yes. I think our sister Grace Anne was the same. I was a little too much for them to handle so before I turned eighteen, my father signed me up for the service to get rid of me." Sin looked at the door again. "Will you be visiting us in Ohio soon, detective?"

"Could. But I'm on assignment here. At least for another year." He looked up the stairs again. "She's something else, isn't she?"

Sin didn't answer. She figured he knew the answer to that. As she went through the door, she spoke again. "Shamus, if you hurt my sister I will kill you."

He threw his arm over her shoulder. "Sin, I think she'll beat you to it. I think your sister is much stronger than you think she is."

Sin thought he might be just the man to make Lilliane believe that too. When she saw her husband stand, she knew that for as long as she lived, she'd never get over the fact that he was hers. And she couldn't wait to let him know about what the big man beside her said. Then she was going to talk to Alyssa about getting Detective McKee assigned to watching over her sister too.

Chapter 5

What do you mean I've been reassigned? I thought I was coming here to be groomed for the position on the homicide force?" Shamus looked at the two men in front of him for answers. When none were forthcoming he turned to his partner Peter. "Well?"

"All I know is they told me to bring you in here. And that, beginning tomorrow, I was training a new guy. I thought," Peter said as he shifted on his seat, "I thought they'd been so impressed with your work so far they already decided to promote you."

Shamus turned back to the men at the desk. "Just where am I headed? Or do I not get that information until I'm there?"

The man on the right, Kendall Dickson his name plate said, shifted and reached for a folder. "You've been assigned special duty to watch over Miss Waite until it can be—"

"Oh no you don't. She is with her family in Ohio. Why can't one of those detectives up there watch over her?" Shamus flushed when Dickson raised his brow. "She'll be just fine where she is. I'm sure she has no intentions of coming back here so I can babysit her," he said in a much more respectful tone.

"Well since I've been told you're going by my boss whose been told by his boss you're going, you're going. End of discussion on that. You leave tonight as a matter of fact. You'll have a group of men to choose from to help with the round the clock set up. A captain…let me see. Ah yes. A Captain Grant is going to assist you in any way you need. She'll have a group of men waiting for you."

"And if I refuse? What then? Do I go back to New York and stay a beat cop for the rest of my career?" Shamus was willing to do that. He didn't want to babysit anyone. Especially a woman like Lilliane Waite.

"No," Gilberto Marsh, the other man at the table, said. "You'll have to turn in your badge. I've been told that if you don't do this assignment then I'm to terminate you. I'm sorry, McKee. Someone had a real hard-on to have you watching this woman. A family like this…hell, boy, they could take you far if you played your cards right."

And then everything fell into place. "The family requested this? I don't suppose you know which one, do you? I'm thinking maybe Alyssa or Cain Waite? Or maybe it was Cooperider on that paperwork."

Shamus was pissed. If little Lillian Waite needed him as a bodyguard then that's what she'd get. He picked up the folder and thumbed through it. There at the bottom of the request was her name. Lilliane I. Waite. He slammed the folder shut and left the office.

He was driving home when he thought of the woman. He'd only seen her twice more before she'd been packed up in the middle of the night and taken home. Her family had been there both times and the second time, her mother and her brother Cain. Cain actually gave Shamus the willies. Sort of the strong silent type with a slow to burn temper. Shamus had seen the temper boiling when Cain had been dealing with his mother.

They'd been fighting, all of them, the first time he'd seen her. The tension had been so thick in the room that it had been tangible. Shamus and Peter had asked a couple of questions more and then left. Cain had called the station to speak to him later that afternoon.

"My mother is upset that…no, that's not right. She's fucking pissed because Lilliane is going home with Alyssa and me. We're letting her stay in our home. I'm sorry if we made you uncomfortable."

"No problem. I don't think she cares all that much for me either." Cain laughed and so did Shamus before he continued. "She is something isn't she, your mom?"

"Yes, that's a nice way of putting she's a bitch." Shamus started to protest. "Don't. I know what she is. But she's still my mother, so short of throwing her out on her ass where she belongs, I simply ignore her as best I can under the circumstances. She hates my wife too."

Shamus didn't know what to say to that so he kept his mouth shut. He wondered now why Cain felt the need to explain or to even call, but maybe his sister had asked for his protection already and Cain was making nice. Either way, Shamus wasn't happy with the situation.

Shamus went back to his hotel, glad now that he'd not had the time to find a house here. He wasn't sure if he'd like Ohio any better, but Nashville had been growing on him. Since he was driving up he packed up his things in his SUV and left within the hour. Peter called just as Shamus was pulling onto the interstate.

"You still pissed off?" Peter sounded amused, which didn't make Shamus any happier. "Could be a worse assignment. Watching over a pretty girl you've been mooning over the past three weeks could be a good thing, you know."

"I have not been mooning over her. She's a victim in a horrific crime, nothing more." But to himself, he knew that kissing her hadn't been enough. "Besides, even if I were, it's not going anywhere now. She's my employer and that's all she'll ever be to me."

Shamus didn't like the bark of laughter that Peter said in answer. "Yeah, that's what they all say. Maybe while you're up there you can figure out the connection between her and the killers. There has to be something. Men just don't pick a girl like her to murder in a mass killing. Not normally anyway. These guys were funded by someone to get her. What I want to find out is what we're missing."

They'd tried every angle too. The trace on the money transfer had hit a dead end. The person who'd given them the money had set it up at the same place the money had been picked up from. They were still trying to figure out who had been the person with the cash and all they'd been able to find was it was either a male or female between the ages of twenty and fifty. Using a very busy terminal had been all the person needed to get the money through.

They couldn't trace the ammo that had been used either. It was a common kind in firepower, which made it difficult. But they'd not been able to find any of it being sold in the quantities that the killers had had. The only thing they could think was either they'd bought it out of state, which it could have been, or they'd bought it in such small quantities and paid in cash that it was nearly impossible to find. The only other thing they'd come up with was that the person who'd wanted Lilliane dead had also supplied the phones, weapons, and ammo to do the job with. And since they couldn't ask the dead men, they couldn't even trace it back to them.

Shamus took his time driving to Ohio. He could have made it in one long trip, but decided to take his time. He no more wanted to do this job than he wanted to lose the one he had so he used the time to think and to calm himself. Shamus got to the hotel he'd planned on staying at until he was finished babysitting or they sent him back to Nashville.

His plan was to set her up then make sure that he never had any direct contact with any of the Waites. He thought he could do it with the help of the captain up here. He would make sure she was covered at all times and he'd be in charge. End of assignment when they figured out they really didn't need him there taking up space and cashing a check. He called Captain Grant as soon as he checked in.

"Are you at the Waite house now? Impressive house, isn't it? I haven't been there as much since Alyssa had the baby, but it's a beautiful house."

"No. I'm at the Marriott on Broad Street where I'll be staying until this is finished. When can I meet the others that you've lined up for this assignment?" He knew they'd been expecting him to stay at the house with her, but he had this under control.

"I thought the plan was for you to stay at the house to guard Lilliane? That's what the orders I got said." Her voice was clipped. "You changing things up isn't going to set well with—"

"I really could care less who I piss off, captain. I do this my way or not at all. I can always reenlist in the service if she gets me fired. So do I meet them here or at your office?" Shamus knew he was talking to his superior, but he didn't like being played.

"I see. Well, if you think you can manage it, come to the station by four today. I'll give you what I have, what we've done, and the security system information at the house where Lilliane is currently staying."

After getting directions to the station house Shamus drove to the closest fast food he could find. Burger King was one of his favorites and he was just sitting down to eat when his cell phone went off.

He almost didn't answer the "unknown," but decided that he'd take a chance on blasting a telemarketer to let off some steam. The voice at the other end of the call was muffled, but clear enough to understand.

"You can't save the cunt. She'll die with the rest of them soon enough." The dial tone sounded long after he realized what the person said.

The French fry he'd been about to eat froze halfway to his mouth. His heart pounded in his chest so hard he thought the next table could hear it. Leaving his untouched burger and drink, he left the restaurant and headed to his car, calling the captain on his way.

"Change of plans. I just got a call on my personal cell from an unknown threatening Miss Waite and the others."

She agreed to meet him at the house and gave him directions to get there. Shamus thought this was not a way to get things going and drove to the house well above the speed limit.

~~~

Lilliane was just settling into the couch her brother had moved her to from the wheel chair when she realized something was up. Sin, as well as Alyssa and Drew, had come into the room with them when she'd said she just wanted to take a short nap. She looked at all of them and was suddenly afraid.

"What is it? What happened now? Is it the babies? Please tell me, you're scaring me."

"First of all," Alyssa started, "nothing has happened. Not yet anyway. But certainly not bad. You'll probably be pissed about it, but I really don't care."

Sin snorted. "Pissed? She's going to be livid and we all know it. I told you we should have told her before he got here. Now it's too late. This was a bad idea and you know it."

"Who got where? What's going on? Sin? Drew? Damn it, Cain, what have you done?" Lilliane had a feeling she wasn't going to like this one bit, more so than Sin had indicated.

"Lilly Pad, we just wanted you to be cared for and happy. And he seemed to—"

She cut Cain off. "Oh my God, you didn't. Please, Cain, please tell me you didn't invite Ward up here to keep me company? I'll kill you—"

"Ward? Ward who? Never mind. I don't want to know." Cain turned to his wife. "You tell her. This was your bright idea anyway. Ward whoever had better not be sleeping with you, that's all I've got to say," he snarled when he turned back to Lilliane.

"I'll sleep with whoever I want whenever I want wherever I want, you overgrown prick. Who made you the sex police anyway? Are you going to stand there and tell me that you and Alyssa didn't have sex before you were married? If you do, I'll know you for a liar." She sat up and threw the blanket off her legs. "I've had enough of this walking around me shit. I'm moving back home as soon as I can arrange it."

Her cell phone she'd just pulled out was snatched from her hand. She looked up at the furious face of last person in the world she'd expected to see here—Shamus McKee.

"Shamus?"

"Yeah, as if you didn't already know I was commanded to be here. You can't go back home just yet, princess. Someone just called a threat on your life again."

She was still trying to believe he was here when she realized what he'd said. Commanded? Her life? Lilliane looked over at Alyssa and knew she'd had something to do with the first part. The second was minor as far as she could see. Who would want her dead? She was a nobody.

She decided she'd speak to her sister-in-law later and turned back to the man towering over her. "You can go back to whatever rock you climbed out from under, Mr. McKee. I don't need you here. I'm quite capable of taking care of myself."

"I'm afraid I can't let you do that, Lilliane. Someone just called Shamus and told him he wouldn't be able to protect you." Lilliane looked over at the doorway where Captain Grant stood with four other men. "Shamus, these are some of the men I've lined up to help you for this. But under the circumstances, I think we should double the amount."

Lilliane looked around the room at the people gathered there and listened to them talk around her. She noticed that no one was paying her any mind so she moved toward the end of the couch and toward her chair. She was just getting into it when Shamus was suddenly there lifting her up.

"Put me down, you idiot. I'm quite capable of getting around on my own. I'm not kidding, Mr. McKee. I've had just about enough of all of you."

"Where's your room?" She glared at him when he asked. Then he turned to Cain. "I'd like a few words with Miss Waite, please. Could you tell me where her room is?"

"I'll take you," the ever helpful Sin said. "She's upstairs. There are quite a few rooms up there so I'll take you."

Lilliane decided to murder Sin in her sleep. She wouldn't be this helpful unless… Lilliane realized that she, too, was in on him being there. She wanted to cry at the way they'd been moving her around like a pawn. No wonder they'd all showed up today; no wonder they'd all been so helpful and sweet. They'd been waiting for him to come.

When she was in her bed, she looked at them both. "Why are you here? You can't have gotten here in the time a call supposedly came to you about me today. So why?"

"You sent for me, princess. It's all here in black and white. Orders to come and play babysitter to one Miss Lilliane I. Waite until further notice. Tell me, what does the 'I' stand for? Innocent? Inculpable? Ingenuous? I know, 'Irreproachable,' seeing how you look so blameless in all this."

"That's enough. You have no right—" Sin snarled at him.

"Shut up, Sin." Lilliane felt the tears burn in her eyes when she looked back at Shamus. "You said you have orders. I'd like to see them, please."

He tossed a folder in her lap and she tried to ignore her shaking fingers as she opened it. It was indeed orders. He'd been assigned to come and guard her until further notice and the name at the bottom alongside Drew's and Captain Grant's was hers.

She held them out to him and when he took them, she looked at her sister, who flushed, and then at Shamus.

"I'd like to be alone. Both of you just get out. I'm…I'm tired and I want to finish my nap that…" She took a deep breath. "Just get out, both of you."

She didn't wait for them to leave, but laid down and rolled to her side, her back to them both. She heard the door close and waited. She wanted to make sure they'd both left before she let go.

She hurt. Not from the injuries, though that was enough, but from what her own twin had done. Lilliane knew she'd been a part of him being there. Sin had looked too guilty not to have been. One thing about being twins like them, Sin and she couldn't hide their emotions from each other.

Chapter 6

It had been two weeks and nothing more. Shamus was also bored and found himself at the station house more often than not. He liked the no-nonsense captain and enjoyed her family a great deal, especially her brother-in-law Jamie. He and the youngest Grant brother were at a bar on Broad Street not far from Shamus' hotel.

"You talked to Lilliane yet?" They'd been avoiding talking about his job, which Shamus had found both welcome and curious. He looked at Jamie when he asked.

"No. She's being protected; that's what I was hired to do and I'm doing it. Cait has been more than helpful getting men lined up to help out and I'm making sure they're at work. Why?"

"No reason," Jamie said with a shrug. "Just seems stupid, that's all."

Shamus knew he was going to hate to ask, but he couldn't seem to stop himself. "Stupid how? And if you suggest that she's a pretty girl and I'm a single man, I'll slug you."

Jamie laughed. He was the most laid back person Shamus had ever met. And from what Jamie had hinted at but never said, he was very wealthy too.

"Nah, wasn't going there. Though I've known the Waite kids most of my life. Cain is a lot of fun and the new husbands can be a blast to hang out with too. My daughter had the biggest crush on Cain when he was younger."

Shamus had met the older Grant child of Jamie's, Deidre Grant. She was a killer in looks and had her mother's gift from what he'd heard. It wasn't like Shamus believed in such things, but it wasn't any of his business.

"I've been coordinating the schedule for Miss Waite. She asked for the help and I'm making sure she gets her money's worth."

That was something he'd not counted on. The money. His tab was being picked up by the Howard Company, and a very substantial one at that, as was his hotel and all his expenses. He'd not expected it and when he'd gone to talk to the owner of the company, he'd been bowled over as if he'd been nothing more than a breath of air.

"Are you not making enough money, Mr. McKee? I can increase your wage if that's what you want."

He looked at Alyssa Waite and frowned. "No, this is nearly three times what I was making as a cop in New York. It's not the money. But just that you shouldn't be paying for it."

"Why? And if you tell me because you don't work for me then you'll have to look at your contract again. You do. What else is it then?"

"I was moved here from my police department not as an employee of Howard but of the Columbus Police. I don't think they'd take too kindly to you—"

She had leaned forward and pressed a button. "Drew, I need you to bring the contract for Mr. McKee please. And bring some water for me. Mine is empty."

A few minutes later, Drew Miller walked in with three bottles of water and a folder. He handed a bottle of water to Alyssa and the folder to him. Shamus was distracted as he watched the woman play with her bottle.

First, she shook it and then checked the seal. As she squeezed the bottle and seemed to examine it for leaks, Drew talked to her as if it was nothing for her to treat the bottle like it was a bomb ready to explode.

"The last shipment of water that came in was from a company I didn't order from. When I tracked down the sender, it was from that ass out in Oklahoma. He said he'd sent it as a gift. I had it sent to the shelter. They'll be careful of its usage." He sat in the chair next to Shamus. "The contract is in there. You work for Howard Enterprise until we end your contract or until the person responsible for the shooting at the school is caught. We pay your wage as we see fit, and expenses. One of the stipulations for you to come here was that the department couldn't afford to pay it. Alyssa wants the best for her family and you're it. As for the other expenses that you should have coming your way, they have been provided; you've just never taken them."

Shamus had looked at the list provided. There was everything a detective, or for that matter, a full department could use to run a large security firm. He looked up at Alyssa and frowned. "I didn't know this was included. I don't even…how did you even get your hands on some of these things? Some of these are so new I don't think they're even available yet to the public."

"They aren't. And don't ask. I have connections you wouldn't believe. Now, we can set them up in your hotel or there is a house that isn't being used on a bit of property that my husband purchased before we met. It's there now. The equipment, I mean. I can have Drew take you there if you'd like, or you can go out on your own."

Alyssa smiled at him and Shamus was sure that she was used to getting her way. He started to tell her he didn't need her ill-gotten gains, but something about Drew clearing his throat stopped him. He was glad he'd stopped when Drew spoke again.

"Lilliane isn't the first Waite to have her life threatened. When Alyssa first met the girls, they were injured in a car accident. My wife was nearly killed in a car crash as well. Sydney, or Sin, was nearly killed when her team was ambushed in Morocco about a year ago and since then we've had minor incidents that we never thought might be connected. Until this thing with Lilliane, we'd only thought they were coincidences. Now…well, now we're not so sure."

"Why wasn't I told about this from the start?" He flushed when he realized why. He'd been avoiding them, all of them, since the day he'd come to Ohio. "Okay, so why now?"

"Because you had a team in place and they seemed to be doing their job. But…well, we're a bit worried about Lilliane. She's…I think she might be up to something and we're not sure what." Alyssa took out a sheet of paper from the top drawer of her desk. "She's not leaving her room until we're all in bed. Ten days ago, a physical therapist showed up at the house and from what I'm told, has been working her very hard to get her into shape. Cain can't get her to tell him anything and the therapist refused to tell. Lilliane told him she'd ruin him if he told anyone what they were doing. HIPAA laws suck when you want information about your family."

Shamus knew about HIPAA or the Health Insurance Portability and Accountability Act, and agreed with it whole heartedly. The sheet Alyssa had handed him was a time table. There were times that the therapist showed up and left. Also, there were a great deal of visits from an attorney named Devin Grant. Shamus wondered if he was related to the captain, but didn't ask.

Shamus came back to the present when Jamie spoke again. "The Grants are a tight family. Well, that would be an understatement. We're like Fort Knox protecting the gold. But the Waites? Well, they've had to watch out for each other. I can remember a time when the elder Waite, Roscoe, had beaten Cain and the kids had stayed with us for a while until the wife could be found. Never seen a bunch of kids that circled the wagons quite like they did. I'm just thinking you could be spending time with them and learning more about what's going on rather than hanging out with an old man like me and drinking beer."

Shamus snorted. Jamie was perhaps ten years older than him if he was that much and the man didn't seem to be in any poor health either. When Jamie winked at him, Shamus laughed.

"You could be right. Hanging out with you has kept me from getting the women, you know. A man in his dotage like you…well, can't be good for a man of my tender years." Shamus laughed and bought another round of beer for the two men.

About twenty minutes later two other men joined the table. Shamus was introduced to Byron and Spencer Grant and decided that he'd been set up. Especially when they were joined by none other than Devin Grant the attorney, and his briefcase.

After two hours with the men, he had a great deal of information on the Waite family, an invitation to stay with Spencer to go fishing, and a invitation to the bondage clubs that Byron owned called Tightly Bound. Shamus' head was reeling when he left the bar later that night. He decided that he needed to talk to Lilliane before too much longer and that tomorrow morning would be just perfect.

~~~

Lilliane could feel the sweat roll down her back. She thought she should have been in better shape than this and if the sadist she'd hired hadn't kept changing the plan daily, she might be. But if the new set of muscles he wreaked havoc on daily was any indication, she'd never be in the shape she wanted.

"Come on now, Miss Lilly, you need to stretch your ass muscles. They are flabby if you ask me. Much too flabby if you want to run a marathon."

She'd told Johnie Griffith, her exercise guru/pain enthusiast, she was running a marathon to explain why she needed help and that her family, overprotective as they were, didn't want her to. She'd also told him numerous times not to call her Lilly. She growled low in her throat before she answered. "I'm not flabby, you masochistic idiot. I'm out of shape. You'd be out of shape too if someone used you as target practice. Now about calling me Lilly, please for the hundredth time, stop calling me that."

"From where I'm standing she doesn't look like she's out of shape either."

Lilliane froze. She knew that voice. She bent further at her waist and looked between her legs at Shamus McKee.

Not bothering to try and hide how much he affected her, hoping the blush of exertion would cover it, she continued with her bends. "The door will lock back on your way out, Mr. McKee. Make sure it doesn't hit your ass too hard when you leave either. Wouldn't want any damage to come to you in my family's home now, would we?"

She flushed deeper when he laughed. She'd meant to piss him off, not have him laugh at her. She bent once more before she moved to the chair. She actually wasn't all that sure she'd be able to move much beyond that. Taking up the towel, she began wiping her face as she tried to ignore him. Christ, he was a gorgeous man.

Tall at what she thought was just over six-foot-six, he towered over even Cain, whom she'd always thought was amazingly tall. Muscles didn't just look like they were a part of him so much as she thought they'd been invented just for him. Dark hair the color she would describe as blue-black and the greenest eyes she'd ever seen. She thought about dark emeralds when she bothered to think about his eyes, which was more often than she wanted. His dark brows slashed over a deep forehead that seemed to be perpetually in a frown and he had a mouth that made her think of sin, sex, and mind-blowing kisses—again, more than she wanted to. She tried to ignore him and continued to talk to Johnie.

"I want to do this again tomorrow if you don't have anything else planned. I have a lot to do and I want to get a good start on it."

"You know," he started in his nasal voice. "You won't get in any better shape if you pull muscles before you begin. I told you that you need to work up to what you want, not do it all in one day."

"Yes, and I'm paying you, not the other way around. Tomorrow, if you please. Eight o'clock if you can be here. I have something to do in the afternoon."

He agreed he'd be here and after he'd pulled a pair of sweat pants over a pair of the skimpiest shorts she'd ever seen, he left. Shamus, of course, only moved into the room and began walking around the exercise equipment she'd had delivered several weeks ago when she decided to hatch this stupid idea. But she wouldn't admit that to him or anyone else for that matter.

"Your family is worried about you. They think you're planning something." She watched as he picked up the barbells she'd used last night, but didn't answer him. "They seem to be under the impression that you're going to run a marathon soon. Is that what this is all about?"

She stood up and wobbled a bit before walking to the bathroom. She closed the door behind her and locked it only to hear him laugh again on the other side of the door. Lilliane leaned heavily against the counter before she looked at her reflection.

She knew she'd lost a lot of weight. Her clothes no longer fit like they had and she could barely keep her underwear up anymore. She leaned closer to see her face. Dark circles marred her cheeks and her hair, dark like Sin's, was now short where she'd taken a pair of scissors to it last week and hacked it all off to about two inches all over. The affect wasn't what she'd wanted, but it didn't hang in her face any more.

Her skin was dry too. So dry that she was surprised each time she took a shower that water actually made it to the drain and her body didn't simply absorb into itself. She decided that she was going to get online and order some lotions tonight and use them more often. She could afford it now.

Selling her little house had been hard. She'd purchased it when she'd gotten the teaching job. But she didn't want to go back there, didn't think she could actually. She'd made a nice, tidy profit off it, and with her savings and the money she'd gotten from her teaching pension she'd cashed in, she thought she could do what she wanted once she escaped from here. Lilliane turned on the shower and stripped down.

Escape was probably a harsh word. She wasn't really a prisoner here, but she'd made herself one. Every day one or more of her family would come by the room to ask her to go somewhere with them—lunch, shopping, even to the library, which was something she really missed. But she couldn't leave. Her whole focus was on getting away. Away from them all and just being Lilliane again.

Once she'd washed her hair and the sweat from her body, she leaned against the tiled wall and let herself feel a bit sorry for herself. The tears she knew were streaming down her face didn't help, but they certainly made her feel less like she was a victim and more like a hurt little girl. She wasn't all that thrilled about either right now. After getting out and drying off, she slathered on the lotion she'd found in the bottom of her case and tried to tell herself she was getting better not worst, but she feared she was only lying to herself. She had to get away.

If she hoped that Shamus would be gone, she was disappointed. He was using her treadmill and was running at what she could only surmise as top speed for the thing. She could barely go twenty minutes on the sucker at low speed and he was running full out and not even breathing hard. He hopped off when he spotted her.

"Nice equipment. I should get me one of them for the house. Might make me feel better about eating out all the time."

She walked to her closet and stepped inside without answering. Closing the door, she blindly reached for some pants and an oversized t-shirt and dressed quickly.

She frowned when he was sitting on her bed when she came out. "I want you to go. I have things to do tonight and they don't involve walking around you."

He simply lay back on her bed as she looked for her shoes. She was on the floor behind the chair when she felt him come up behind her. She hated the way she flinched before she'd realized who he was and felt even more stupid when he frowned at her.

"You're still scared about the shooting. Understandable. I would have thought that your family would have insisted on therapy for you by now. It's very hard being shot at."

She wanted to ask who'd shot at him, but didn't. When he didn't back up so she could get up, she simply crawled forward and moved the chair as she went. He picked her up by the waist and she stumbled back against him before she could think. When she tried to get away, he pulled her closer.

"Let me go. I don't need, nor do I want your assistance." She tried again to get away only to be held still. "Do you mind?"

"Not really. You feel good against my body. There was a time when you would have welcomed my kisses and touching you. What happened?"

"You did. Now let go." This time when she pulled away he let her, but he didn't leave. "I want you to go. Your men are doing what I hired them to do, now go."

He sat on the chair she'd been moving around looking for her shoe. Frustrated, she sat on the bed and pulled on her shoe. She ignored his offer of help.

"I know you didn't send for me." She looked up sharply when he said that. "I also know that you didn't know I was coming until I got here. You should have told me."

She wanted to tell him that he wouldn't have believed her anyway, but pulled her other shoe on. She had no idea why she was putting on her shoes; she'd not left this room in over a week, even taking her meals up here.

"Not talking to me, huh? That's fine. I'll do the talking. I also found out that you're not the only member of your family that has been attacked." She paused in tying her shoe. "And that your family has had some really rough times over the past two years or so from the accidents."

"What the hell does this have to do with your being here now? Nothing. It was a school shooting. I was shot and others…others were killed. I'm going to move on and I suggest you do the same." She stood up and walked to her door. "I want you to get out of here. I don't have anything else to say to you."

He took his time standing and when he reached the door she let out a breath, happy he'd decided to listen to her. But it was short lived when he took the door from her and closed it. Before she could open her mouth to scream at him he had her pressed against the door and his mouth over hers.

Chapter 7

He hadn't meant to kiss her. He'd only meant to make her understand that things were going to be different now. But seeing her standing within inches of him had his cock surge in his jeans and he wanted her. So he took.

Her mouth was soft and firm at the same time. He could feel her stiffen when he'd put his hand on her waist, but when he lifted it to her breast, she'd moaned. Shamus felt like she'd given him a gift and he wasn't going to go away until he'd tasted more of her. Moving his thigh between her legs, he'd just begun to lift her over him when he felt the pain radiate around his groin. As the pain blossomed and grew he pulled back and looked down at her. Her smile of satisfaction had him groan and then his body clenched in pain.

"Damn it," he growled at her as he fell to the floor. "That fucking hurt." After that all he could do was lay there until the pain went away. She simply stepped over him and out the door and there wasn't a damned thing he could do about it. For now, at least.

As the pain receded he thought of all the things he was going to do to her when he got up. First and foremost was kissing her again. He'd be more careful for sure, but he'd damn well do it. He was just beginning to feel his legs again when he heard someone laughing and tilted his head a bit to see Cain standing nearby.

"She left her room. I was wondering why when I realized that she was pissed. So I thought I'd come and see what she'd done now. I'm sorry to say I wasn't expecting to see a man on the floor of her room except maybe that Johnie person, but you? Never."

Shamus growled. "She kicked me. Then she didn't even have the decency to give me a pillow or a bag of ice. She's going to pay for this."

Cain laughed again, reached down, and looked into Shamus' eyes. "She hurt you other than your nuts?"

"No, and would it hurt you at all to be the least bit sympathetic about this? She could have done some permanent damage to me." Shamus rolled to his back and glared up at Cain who was laughing again. "You're going to pay too."

"Nah, she didn't hurt anything but your pride. Well, maybe your jewels for a bit, but nothing that won't recover. You must have been pretty close to her to get you that good. What were you doing to her?"

Shamus answered before he thought. "I was kissing her. And she was kissing me back before she nailed me with her knee."

That shut up her brother. Shamus might have laughed at the abrupt change in temperament if Cain didn't look ready to murder him. Shamus stiffened his body, ready for whatever the man had, when suddenly Alyssa was there too.

"Behave or I'll tell him about the time I did the same to you. Are you all right, Shamus, or do I need to call Damon? He'll most certainly treat you better than Cain will right now."

Shamus shook his head, but didn't take his eyes off the standing man. He figured that Cain was either going to finish what his sister didn't or simply shoot him where he lay. Either way, Shamus was going to fight back. What he didn't expect was the man to put out his hand and laugh.

"I taught Lilly Pad that when she was sixteen and some boy at school wouldn't stop trying to…well, he wanted more than she was willing to give. Shut him right up too." Shamus stood as Cain continued. "It's not going to work with you, is it?"

Honesty seemed the best route at this point so Shamus looked Cain in the eye. "No. Not on me it won't. But I won't hurt her and I do know the meaning of the word 'no.' But I would like to hear it before she tries to do me in again."

Cain nodded and they both turned to look at Alyssa who was clapping her hands. "Bonding is so sweet when it's between two grown men."

"You,"—Cain pointed at her—"I can spank. And I will if you don't behave. Shamus kissed Lilly Pad and she unmanned him. What should we do about that?"

Before Shamus could tell the man to butt out Alyssa beat him to it. "We aren't going to do anything. You are going to stay out of it and I'm going to make sure you do. I mean it, Cain. I'd hate to have to cut you off if you don't behave yourself."

"But, Alyssa, she left her room and she—"

"Cain." The single word came out a long syllable that had Cain closing his mouth with a snap. "Now, let's go eat the Chinese food we ordered and keep whatever thoughts are circling around your head to ourselves, shall we? Shamus, would you like to join us? There will be plenty, I'm sure."

Shamus nodded. He was actually afraid that if he opened his mouth the laughter spilling from it would get him hurt. Cain seemed to know this and kept glaring at him. Shamus was all the way down the stairs before he realized that he'd not spoken to Lilliane like he'd planned. But he did ask if he could move into the vacant house that had been mentioned before.

"Sure," Cain said. "I know that it's empty at the moment. Jazzie was staying there for a little while, but she recently moved into her own apartment when Sin got married. I think it's got some of your stuff in it anyway."

"Captain Grant said she'd sent some equipment there a few weeks ago and Devin Grant said he had things ready as far as Internet and things set up. He seemed to think you wouldn't mind."

"Yeah, I signed for it all, but honestly, I forgot all about it until now. What is it anyway? Police stuff?" Cain seemed to pluck his son from mid air when it looked like he was going to tumble onto his head and didn't miss a beat in the conversation they were having either. "I wouldn't mind having a look at it. It's always fascinated me what kind of equipment the department uses to get the bad guy."

The dining room table was huge, as was the entire house. There was a long table set for at least twenty people and what looked like brown paper bags filled with enough food to do so. Lilliane was just sitting down at one of the middle chairs with a baby in her arms when Shamus entered.

She looked so…well, he supposed natural would have been the right word, but it seemed to be so much more. She held the baby like she'd been born to do so. Her face looked like she was enjoying it as well. When Quinn, one of her other sisters, handed her a bottle, she gave it to the baby like a pro and had Shamus feeling things he'd never thought of before. At least until she spotted him. As she started to rise Alyssa put her hand on her shoulder and whispered something in her ear that had her sitting back down. He wondered what had changed her mind and decided he'd ask Alyssa later.

"Come on, everyone. Fix yourself a plate. Shamus, sit there, and Cain, how about you open the wine? Sin and Payton will be here shortly, something about a drunk driver on Main Street. Quinn, where's Drew?" Alyssa had everyone organized and seated before the first bag was opened.

"He'll be along soon. He had to pick up something for you at the court house, he said." Quinn handed him a baby and a bottle as she spoke. Shamus just looked at it. "His name is James. And he'll enjoy that bottle more if you put it in his mouth."

Shamus looked at Quinn, who winked and motioned for him to put the bottle in the baby's mouth. As soon as the nipple was near his mouth, the kid latched onto is like he'd been starved. He said as much out loud.

"I was nursing him for a little while, him and the other two, but he would never seem to be full. I swear he's like this eating machine. He's not as hungry now as he's been, but he still goes at it like it's his last meal." Shamus laughed with the rest of the table. A plate was set before him before he could think to ask what they had.

"Just eat what you want. I'm sure there is more than enough to choose from when you get that one finished," Cain said. "When he's done, I'll take him from you and burp him. I'm the only one who can get him to do it with gusto."

The banter around the table centered mostly on the babies and the raising of them in sets or singles. The babies, five of them now, were a bundle of energy when not sleeping and if not for the nannies and other help, none of them would have made it past the first month Payton told Shamus when he got there.

Sin's little girl Tonya was named after a friend of her mother, Tonya Carol. Tonya was adopted, he'd learned, and Sin and Payton were expecting to be able to adopt another little boy soon. They were unable, it seemed, to have their own children, yet seemed just as loving and happy with their adopted daughter as either of the other two families with their own.

Quinn had a set of triplets. Two boys, Thomas and James, and a little girl, Abida Rose, were spitting images of their mother. The little girl seemed to know she was going to be a diva and had her daddy wrapped tightly around her finger too.

She didn't make a sound when she was burped, but made this little noise much like a purr that had Shamus laughing. The boys, rough and tumble even so young, seemed to take great pride in their lives already. Shamus got James to not only burp, but to do it three times before he fell asleep in his arms.

Connor, the oldest of the babies, sat on his daddy's lap and picked at his plate like a pro. Cain didn't seem to notice the rice that spilled down his front nor the little bit of drool on his arm when Connor zonked out with the rest of the kids. When a nanny came to gather them up and take them to the nursery Shamus dug into his food. He glanced over at Lilliane when she pushed her half full plate back.

"You need to eat more. You're much to skinny as it is. And the calories you're burning with your exercise isn't near what you ate."

"Mind your own business," she hissed at him. "I know what I'm doing. And who asked you anyway?"

He leaned close to her, mindful of the others around the table, and whispered in her ear. "I'm making it my business to get you healthy because I plan to get you beneath me before too much longer. I want to feel you surrounding me when you come and I want to taste your cream as soon as I can get you naked." He nipped at her earlobe before pulling back.

Her mouth opened and closed several times before she turned away from him. He thought he'd seen a flicker of need race across her face, but couldn't be sure. What he was sure of was that he wanted her, wanted this woman above all else right now. When she stood he knew she was going to bolt, and he didn't have a clue how to keep her there.

When she left the room without a word everyone turned to him. He felt his face heat with embarrassment and something he'd not felt since he was a kid. Shame. Before he could open his mouth and tell them he was sorry, Drew smiled.

"Are you going after her? Speaking from experience here, the Waite women can be quite...willing if you make them understand you're not giving up."

Shamus looked at Cain. "I didn't mean to—"

"This isn't getting her. Go." As Shamus stood, Cain stopped him as he continued. "You hurt her, I will kill you."

Shamus nodded once and left the room. He heard Alyssa saying something to her husband about leaving witnesses but didn't care. He was going after Lilliane and damn the consequences.

~~~

Lilliane dropped her shirt on the floor as she entered the room. Her bra, a sports one, was about all she'd worn since she'd come home from the hospital and she didn't think to put on anything different when Shamus had come to her room. Now she was glad she had. The sweat pants were next. And they slid to the floor easily because nothing fit like it should. She plugged the key into the treadmill before she was even on it.

Running away wasn't an option at the moment, but she could run. When the machine started up, it nearly knocked her back it was going so fast, but she caught up quickly. Run, was all she could think right now. Run and don't think about the man downstairs.

He wanted her. No, that wasn't what he'd said. He said he wanted her beneath him. An easy lay, someone he could sate his lust with. She nearly laughed out loud at that because she wasn't the type that men did those sorts of things to. She was the girl men talked to, endlessly.

When something grabbed her around the waist, she screamed and then was flipped around. Shamus had the tiny key in his hand and her in his other. Her heart was pounding so hard she knew he could hear it.

"I'm not in the mood to be around you right now. I want you to go away and leave me alone like you were. The other men were doing just fine keeping me out of trouble." She tried to turn from him, but he pressed her against the column of the now quiet treadmill.

"No." He cupped her ass in his palm and lifted her up against his hips even as he took her mouth.

His mouth wasn't warm and soft like when he'd kissed her before. It was demanding, hot, and oh-so delicious. As much as she wanted to make him stop, make him leave her alone, all she could think of was touching him, having him do the things he'd talked about down at the table.

When the bed was under her, she moaned. The contrast between the cool, soft spread beneath her and the hot, hard man over her was too much and yet not enough. She wrapped her legs around his hips even as he bit into her breast. Every nerve in her body seemed to come alive with the sharp pain-pleasure he gave her. Surging up, she nearly screamed out when he bared her breast and took her soft flesh into his mouth.

Lilliane could feel his cock pressed between her thighs and wanted to feel him against her skin. Reaching down between them she cupped her hand around him and when he rocked against her, she felt power surge through her veins. Need, she needed this man, needed him in a way she'd never known, never felt before. When he moved to her other breast, she tried to work his pants open to touch.

"Are you on the pill?" The question startled her for a moment. When he repeated it, his voice deep and heavy with something, she nodded.

The pill? Birth control—yes, that's what he meant. Her panties were suddenly gone, her bra lifted up and over her head, and Shamus was sitting on his knees between her legs.

Lilliane leaned up on her elbows and watched as he unbuttoned his shirt. He never said anything, just slowly moved the tiny button through each hole as he watched her. When the shirt was undone she licked her lips as he took it off and tossed it to the floor beside the bed. She watched it pool on the floor.

She looked back at him when he shifted on the bed. His chest was lightly furred, covered in a dark hair that went from nipple to nipple and then trailed down his body to his pants. She leaned forward to run her fingers through it and was stopped when his hand covered hers. She looked up into his face.

"If you touch me much more, I'm not going to last. And I desperately want to taste you." She nodded at him, ready to agree to anything so long as he touched her again. "Lay back. Let me love you with my mouth."

Her body tightened and she felt the cream that had been there before gush from her. She tried to close her legs to hide what she'd felt and he wrapped his hands around her thighs and opened her. After telling her to lay back again, she did and tired not to think about how much of her he was seeing.

"Beautiful. You're so beautiful I can't wait to taste you." As he moved back on the bed she thought he was going to leave her there, but when he leaned down and kissed her pelvic bone just above her curls, she moaned deep in her throat.

The first flick of his tongue nearly sent her off the bed; his low chuckle had her burn with embarrassment. She tried to pull away again, but suddenly his mouth was over her and his finger deep inside of her.

"Shamus," she cried out as her body surged up. Every time she moved he was there, deep inside of her. Suckling her, taking her to such heights, then pulling her back down again. His tongue filled her even as his finger did. She found herself riding him, his mouth, his finger, anything she could to make whatever was just out of her reach come.

The climax was close, so close she knew that once she hit it, nothing would ever be the same. Her fingers tangled in his hair, guiding him to where she wanted. Her legs lifted up and encircled his neck, using his body to ride more of his wonderfully talented mouth.

Begging him now, begging him for what she knew only he'd ever be able to give her, she felt his finger slide up the crack of her ass and circle her tight anus. She wasn't sure if she was trying to get away or wanted more when he slid into her. When he did, she came apart.

Stars. She not only saw them, but felt them sprinkle down over her body and touch her. Tiny fusions of heat infused her with sensations. She wanted more, she wanted less, her body on fire like a house fire gone mad. When Shamus settled between her legs again, he kissed her. Passion. Fire and something more. Something that felt both out of control and yet comforting at once. Then he was inside of her.

She couldn't stop the scream of pain. Lilliane tried to move, to try and get away from the burning and the hurt. Taking deep breaths, she realized that Shamus was speaking…well, cussing was more like it.

"Mother fucking…son of a bitch. Fucking stupid…of all the fucking—why the fuck didn't you say something before? I would have…"

When he didn't finish, she turned to look at him then quickly away again. "Would have what? What would you have done? Never mind. I want you to leave. Right now, just leave."

He turned her head to his again and looked down at her. She felt the tears fall down her cheeks and tried to turn away again, but he held her still. She closed her eyes, not wanting to see his disappointment there. His next words shocked her into opening her eyes again.

"I would have been more careful. I would have taken more care with your virginity. You should have told me." While he didn't sound mad really, he did sound concerned. "We can stop now if you want."

She nodded her head and shifted under him. The sensation was overwhelming and she moved again. When he laughed, she looked at his face.

"It's not so bad now. If you want to finish…if you need to finish up then go ahead." She tried to look away when he laughed again, but he pulled her back. "You don't have to make it okay for me. I know men need only to…"

"Need only to what," he asked her when she didn't finish. "What do you think men need, Lilliane?"

"To have a body. Don't you? Need just a body to enjoy yourself? I mean, I know some about sex even if I've never done it before. I'm not stupid." She didn't have any idea why she was pissed, but she found she really was. "Just finish up so you can leave."

"I don't think so. And for the record, men don't even need a body to 'finish up,' as you put it. Our hand will do nicely in a pinch." He rocked into her again and she felt her body tingle. "You want me to finish you up while I'm at it?"

He was making fun of her. The tears that had been there before fell again and she didn't even try to hide them from him. She pushed at his shoulders, not even moving him the slightest bit when she'd put all her strength into it.

"Get off me." And when he rolled to his back, taking her with him, she found herself suddenly over him, his body beneath her.

Chapter 8

Shamus had never taken a woman's virginity before. But he'd be damned if he'd let this one tell him he could finish without her. He looked up into her bright eyes and realized that even if he lived another fifty years and took another dozen women to his bed, this one, this tiny woman, would always hold a special place.

"Ride me. Move your body over mine and ride me." He watched the confusion mar her pretty face. Cupping his hands over her hips, he moved her, showing her what he meant. It didn't take her long to figure it out and she was going to kill him before this was over.

Lifting her hands up, he lifted her breasts up with his hands beneath hers. She was so lost in the way her body was enjoying his that he knew she didn't have any idea what she was doing to him. As she began to massage her breasts, lifting them up and then pinching her nipples, she threw back her head and picked up her pace. Shamus was mesmerized by the way she looked so that when she began to ride him in earnest he leaned up, took her nipple in his mouth, and nipped it.

Her climax shattered her. He watched every breath she took, gasping for air even as she cried out. Her breasts flushed a deep red and her nipples hardened more. When she leaned forward and dug her nails deep into his chest, he rolled her to her back and pumped into her deep.

"Come again, baby. Let me feel your tight sheath milk me again. Feel you clamp me tight while I come deep inside of you. Come, Lilliane, come for me."

With her eyes wide open, she cried out his name again. Shamus had never felt such a connection before, a connection so deep that he felt himself tumble right after her and knew that he'd never be the same.

Rolling to his back again, he took her with him and settled her lax body over his. Shamus knew he'd probably hurt her again, but couldn't for the life of him drum up the worry about her being upset with him. She'd come and come hard. Twice, as a matter of fact, well before he had. He smiled when she snuggled up under his chin and didn't move.

But as he lay there he began to think, and he knew that if he stayed where he was, he'd either end up making love...no, having sex with her again or pissing her off. He waited until she was asleep before he began to work himself out from under her. When he was sitting on the side of the bed, he looked back at her.

Her neck was burned from his whiskers. He reached up and rubbed his hand over the hard bristles and decided that he'd shave before taking her again. Just as that thought completed, he leapt from the bed and jerked on his briefs. He turned his back on her, refusing to look at her.

Women like her, he thought, virgins like Lilliane, didn't do one night stands like him. He wanted her again, he even thought about climbing back in beside her and taking them both to the heavens again, but he didn't. Pulling his shirt on, he was buttoning it up as he made a grab for his shoes. Sitting down and pulling them on, he glanced over at her.

She looked so lovely lying there. So serene and relaxed. His cock hard even though he'd just had sex, incredible sex, surged against the zipper and made him groan in pain. Yeah, he needed to get involved with her like he needed a hole in his head. He was nearly down the stairs when he realized she was going to get him fired. At this point, he'd welcome it.

~~~

Cain watched Shamus leave. He would have called out to him, but something made him stop. He looked up the stairs at where his sister was and then back at the closed door. Something had happened. Cain turned to his wife when she came up behind him and put her arm around his waist.

"You can't help her with this, Cain. And hunting him down won't solve anything either. They'll either work it out or they won't. Stay out of it."

Cain put his hand over her arm and leaned back to her. "I want to go up and see that she's okay, but I don't think I can handle it if they had sex and she's still…well, she's still…you know."

"Naked? Probably. But stay down here with me. She'll be fine. Lilliane is a lot stronger than any of you give her credit for. She'll be fine. And if not, and only if she asks, will we give her any help. Besides," she said as he turned in her arms. "We have a few hours to ourselves while Connor is down for a nap. Wanna fool around?"

Cain was nodding even as he took her mouth. Kissing her and moving her back against the wall seemed as good as place as any to start making love to his wife. He felt his phone seconds before it went off and he groaned as he pulled back. "I'm on call. I have to take this." When she growled, he nearly tossed the phone across the room but answered it instead. Before he could say his name, the person started talking.

"You can't save her. I'm going to get her and the rest of them before I take that pretty wife of yours and kill them all. And then you."

The room seemed to shrink in size then expand before he could breathe again. He knew that he was holding a dead line even before he looked at the phone and saw a picture of his wife and son on the front before it went black. He looked at Alyssa and then pulled her to him.

"Don't speak. I… Someone just threatened you all. All of us. I'm going to let you go soon. I think. And then I want you to call Shamus and Cait." He tried to make himself let Alyssa go, but he couldn't quite seem to make his fingers work. "I can't lose you, none of you."

"Cain, what did they say? Let me go, honey. Let me go so I can call Shamus back." Her voice sounded too distant, but he did let her go enough to look at her. "Cain, what did they say?"

"That I couldn't save her. That I couldn't save any of us." He took a deep breath and let it out slowly. "Call them."

The next hour was a nightmare. The police arrived just seconds after Shamus did. And then a group of men arrived from Alyssa's office to start walking the perimeter. Cain watched everything from the dining room table, as it seemed everyone was asking questions. It wasn't until he realized that someone was putting a drink in his hand that he saw Payton standing before him and no one else. He looked at his brother-in-law.

"They volunteered me to sit with you. I guess they figured if you went ape-shit, I could tackle you." Payton sat on the chair next to him. "Tell me what they said word for word."

Cain looked around. He knew he'd told his wife, but he didn't want his family to know. "That I couldn't save her. That they were going to get her and the rest of them before whoever it was takes my pretty wife and kills them all. And then me. Then the person hung up."

Payton stood and went to the doorway where Cain noticed that Shamus was standing. When Payton asked if Shamus could come in, Cain nodded. The numbness was starting to wear off and he was beginning to get pissed.

"Cain, what can you tell me about the person?" Cain must have looked confused because Shamus started again. "Did you notice if it was a male or female? An accent or some word that didn't sound right?"

"No. The voice sounded…muffled. Maybe even like it was in a tunnel or something. Or speaking through a towel. Yeah, through a towel like the person wanted to hide his or her voice from me." He was actually proud of that thought until he looked at Shamus. "What? What is it?"

"I had the same feeling when they called me. What about background noises? Think, were there car noises? Something you might have not realized that you heard and was there? Close your eyes and listen to the voice again, but soften it, make it less important than the things in the background."

Cain closed his eyes and brought up the voice again. It was hard at first; the words the person used terrified him. He couldn't lose his family. Then as he heard the soft tones in Shamus' voice, he concentrated less on the words like he'd asked and more on what he didn't hear.

"There's a horn. Like a blast from a car when you cut them off. A bark of a cuss word. 'Fuck' or 'truck,' I think. Not from the person who called, but…it sounded like it was farther away." Cain opened his eyes to see Shamus taking notes. "Is that helpful?"

Shamus nodded. "Yes. The person was driving probably and it was with others around so they probably did this call spur of the moment. The windows on the car were also probably open, meaning they weren't going all that fast."

"How do you know that?" Cain looked at Payton when he laughed.

"It's too fucking cold to be on the interstate with the windows open, but perfect for a nice ride through town." Payton looked at Shamus as he continued. "You're damn good at this. How long you been in homicide?"

"I'm not." Cain noticed the bite in Shamus' words, but before he could comment, Shamus continued. "There's been a threat on all the families' lives but yours. I think it's because you fall apart when your sisters and your wife are threatened. And whoever is doing this knows it."

Cain wanted to be pissed about the comment about falling apart when Payton took over for Shamus. "Also, you're male. The men, they've not been threatened unless they're with the women when they're harmed. Could be that they just want your family dead and not so much the in-laws."

Shamus got up to pace as Sin came into the room. "Lilliane is outside with three guards. She said she wanted some air and as this place is like a prison, I told her not to leave the grounds. Tomorrow, I'm showing her how to use a gun."

None of the men said anything to Sin when she made this statement, but Cain noticed that Shamus seemed to stiffen. Cain had a second to wonder about that, but his son came crawling into the room about then and he bent to scoop him up and hold him close.

"The children. She never mentioned the children. Why is that, you think?" Cain looked at Shamus again when he stopped pacing. "What now? You know, you're sort of creepy when you do that."

"She, you said she. Tell me right now what is going through your mind to make you think it was a she."

Cain blurted out his answer before he could think. "Because a man would have been more direct. A woman needs to plan."

Sin snorted. "Of course we would. And we'd do it right the first time too." All three men looked at her and she flushed. "I'm sorry, that came out all wrong."

Cain watched Payton pick up his wife and sit her on his lap. It was extremely disconcerting to watch any of his sisters with another man, especially Sin. She was the baby and would always be five in his eyes. He looked away when they started kissing. Yeah, too much, he thought.

As more people began to filter in and out of the room, Alyssa seemed to be making sure that everyone was being cared for. Coffee urns had been set up and he could see a vegetable plate being set out. At some point, someone must have ordered pizza because there was a shout that the pizza boy was clean. Cain had a thought as to how much they searched the poor kid before they let him go and how much therapy he was going to need to get over this.

He stood up and looked out the window in time to see Lilliane sitting in the swing that they'd had put in recently for the kids. She looked so sad that Cain grabbed up his jacket then reached in for one for her and headed out to the lawn. She was crying softly when he got to her.

Handing her the jacket, he waited for several seconds before he spoke. "I can't let anything happen to you, Lilly Pad. You and the other girls…you're my life. You have to know that'll I'll protect you."

The creak of the swing sounded before she spoke. "Yes, I know. But you have to know that I can't let anything happen to you either. You're the only man in my life that I love and besides, Alyssa would hurt you if you died."

He laughed and turned to her. Her face was tear-streaked and her nose was red. He pulled her from the swing and held her. For several minutes, neither of them said a word.

"I tried to save those children. I wanted to make sure…they died because of me." He started to protest when she hushed him with a hand over his mouth. "You know as well as I do that those men came there to kill me. And they planned to kill all of those children as well. How can I ever forgive myself for that?"

He moved her hand down from her mouth and answered her. "You are the best person in the world and if it hadn't been

75

for you, all of them, every child and adult in that building would have died. But they didn't count on you fighting back. They didn't count on a Waite being on the other side of that door and willing to give her all in saving those that she could. Lilliane, you didn't cause their deaths. You had nothing to do with either those men nor the person that is trying now. You saved all of them."

He held her longer as she cried softly. After a few minutes he saw Jazzie coming toward them and, when she was close, she wrapped her arms around the two of them. He went into the house when one of the police told him that his phone was ringing. As much as he hated to leave them, he knew that even with all of Jazzie's quirks, she'd take care of Lilliane.

Chapter 9

Jazzie watched Cain walk away. She waited until he was inside the house before she spoke quietly to her sister. She and Lilliane had been planning this for weeks and now was the time to act. She wasn't thrilled about the plan Lilliane had come up with, but she understood completely.

"I have your money. It came this morning." Lilliane pulled back to look at her. "Are you sure this is a good idea? I mean, with all these cops around, wouldn't everyone be safe if you stayed anyway?"

Lilliane sat on the swing as Jazzie took the other one. "Would you? Would you stay if it meant some crazed person coming in and shooting up the place with everyone here?"

Jazzie knew that she would have left too. But she didn't want her sister alone either. She looked over at Lilliane, trying once more to convince her to stay now.

"What about that detective? Won't he be upset with you? I mean, you're sleeping with him, right?" Jazzie looked back at the window where she could see the man she was talking about. "He looks like he can keep you safe."

"I think something happened between the time he left my bed and now." Jazzie snorted at her sister. "I mean between us," Lilliane said with a blush.

"Like what? He wants to do it again and you don't want to? What happened besides the world crashing down around us all?" Jazzie looked at her sister when she didn't answer right away. She could see the way she looked up at the window and wondered if her sister was in love with the big man. She started to ask when Lilliane spoke.

"He won't look at me. Not only that, but when I went to him after Cain called the police, he pulled away from me and told me that he had to talk to me later. I asked him what and he said he might have…he said he thought maybe we should slow things down a bit. That he'd put the horse before the cart and wanted to rectify that."

Jazzie stared at Lilliane. "You're kidding? He wants to…what is it he wants to slow down?" Then dawning hit her. "You were a virgin, weren't you, and now he feels guilty about it?"

"Yes, and I suppose. He didn't seem all that upset about it when…when we…you know. He even told me that he'd have taken better care not to hurt me." Lilliane sighed before she continued. "I guess he had second thoughts."

Jazzie pulled the large brown envelope out of her coat pocket and gave it to her. She didn't know what to say other than beg her not to go, but she knew her sister well enough to know that once she made up her mind, she stuck with it. They sat in the swings for a few minutes more before Jazzie asked her what she knew she wouldn't get an answer for.

"Will I know where you are? Where you're going?" The negative reply was soft and just what she expected. "I won't know how to reach you, will I? I won't know if you're dead or alive. How will I know if this person hasn't gotten you?"

Lilliane stood and turned her back to the window. "Do you remember Devin Grant?" Lilliane asked. When Jazzie nodded, Lilliane went on. "He'll contact you every other week a month from now. I've already sent him the notice that I would be contacting him. He's to let you know what I tell him."

Jazzie stood up too. "I didn't know you were…you're going now, aren't you? Tonight?"

With a quick hug, Lilliane stepped back. "I love you, Jaz, more than anything in this world. Tell Cain…tell him I'm sorry." And then without a backward glance, Lilliane walked away.

Jazzie sat back down in the swing, knowing that as soon as she went inside she'd have to explain why Lilliane wasn't with her. Setting the ride in motion, she swung her feet back and forth until she was soaring through the sky and back again. She only wished her heart didn't feel so broken.

When she started to slow, she looked at her watch and figured that Lilliane would be to the second point of her escape by now as an hour had passed. Standing up, Jazzie straightened her clothes and walked slowly toward the door. She decided that whoever she saw first was who was going to learn first. She hoped it would be Alyssa, but with her luck, she just knew it was going to be her brother. But she was wrong on both. It was Shamus.

"Where's your sister? She shouldn't be out there this late. Maybe you could please tell her to come inside now."

Taking a deep breath and wishing now she'd waited for Cain, she told him what Lilliane had made her practice telling them. "She's gone. She won't be coming back." Jazzie wanted to say more, wanted to ask him what he'd done to her to hurt her sister, but she only repeated what she'd been told to say. "She's gone. She won't be coming back."

~~~

Shamus stared at the note in front of him. It had been delivered just over thirty minutes ago and an hour after Jazzie had shared that her sister had run. He read it again.

"This is for the best. If the person returns to finish what they started, the children and you, my family will be safe. Don't blame Jazzie or ask her what she knows. She only knew that I wanted the money delivered to her house and nothing more until I told her goodbye."

Not even a damned signature. Shamus looked up when Cain came back into the room. He'd been ranting for the past hour and he looked like he had a full head of steam under him this time.

"The airport has no report of her taking a flight out. Either she's still in town or took another mode of transportation out. Which is it? You are the big, bad cop; tell me where my sister is."

Shamus raised a brow at the title, but didn't answer. When he'd tried answering Cain before when the note had been first delivered, the man practically tore his head off. Cain didn't want answers, he wanted solutions. And Shamus was wallowing in too much guilt to have any right now.

He knew that her leaving like she had was probably due to his treatment of her earlier. He'd been cold, but he'd been scared. He was no less scared, but he knew that he should have handled things between them a little differently. When Cain left the room again, Shamus leaned in his chair and buried his head in his hands. He heard someone come into the room and close the door and he waited for Cain to rant some more. When nothing was forthcoming, he looked up and groaned. He so didn't need Guinevere right now.

"Do you know where the girl went? I'm her mother and you need to tell me." Shamus was reasonably sure that she actually expected him to tell her. Even if he did know, he wouldn't be telling her. There was something not quite right about this woman.

"I don't know," is all he said.

She huffed at him and sat on the chair next to his. "She's always been a willful child. I never could understand what she was thinking when she ran off when Sydney Valeria did. Not one of my children have any respect for me, especially now that their father was murdered by that horrible woman in the other room."

Shamus had heard bits and pieces of the story from the others. Roscoe had kidnapped his eldest child over some money. What Shamus didn't understand was why Guinevere even stayed around when she so obviously hated her children. Okay, maybe hate was too harsh, but she definably didn't know him. She was still speaking when Shamus thought to grill her.

"…a mess of everything now that she's got her claws into him."

Shamus knew she was referring to Alyssa by the way she had sneered the title when saying it. Shamus only nodded. Sometimes, like now, it was just easier to do that than to try and figure out why a person felt the way he or she did about someone. But he had to admit, something was going on. He thought he'd try a different approach.

"So what does your husband's death have to do with Mrs. Waite?" He knew the second she glared at him he'd done well to call Alyssa Mrs. Waite. Angry people tended to forget to hold their tongue.

"She's a money-grubbing whore. If she would have paid up when she knew she should have, none of this would be happening."

Shane frowned. "None of what? I don't understand."

Guinevere stared at him for several seconds, her face a complete blank, then when she answered, he had an idea what she said wasn't what she'd intended to say. "Why my Roscoe would be alive and he'd protect his girls, that's all. None of this would have been going on because my Roscoe would have eliminated the problem to begin with."

Cain came in just then with a huge smile on his face. "You have to see this, Shamus. You're not going to believe it."

Shamus stood to follow Cain, feeling that he was missing something. Something vital and important. And he planned soon to come back and dig deeper into this conversation. But he followed Cain. He could use a good dose of humor right now.

Everyone was standing in the kitchen looking out the large glass wall that was the focal point in the breakfast nook that spilled into the yard. By the time he'd made his way to the front he'd gotten snippets of information. Grace Anne, the last sister, was finally home. And apparently, she'd brought home someone with her. When Shamus could make out who it was, he burst out laughing.

There in the side yard stood another beautiful Waite woman. Short tumble of dark curls mussed from what Shamus noticed by her hand slicking it back out of her face. She was sleek, slim, and incredibly pissed if her arms swinging had anything to say about it. Even in her very nice clothes, the woman was screaming like a fisherwoman at the person standing across from her. And Lilliane was not standing there taking it either.

The heated expression on Lilliane's face was simply beautiful. Shamus was sure that he'd never seen anyone so angry before. Well, except for the woman she was fighting with. He turned to Cain as the man came up beside him.

"Should we go out and break it up? While I'm sure Lilliane is strong enough to take the other one on and come out a winner, the men might get an eyeful if either of them take a tumble in the dirt."

Shamus laughed out loud at Cain's heavy sigh. "Yeah, I suppose. But just so you know, if I have to help physically pull them apart, then you get Gracie. She's meaner than a wet hen when she's pissed off. And she doesn't fight fair, even for a girl."

Shamus ended up with the bloodied nose that Cain laughed about every time he looked over at him. Shamus had finally had to go into the smaller living room just to get away from the man.

Gracie was mean, as it turned out, but Shamus got the bloodied nose from Lilliane. As far as he was concerned, she didn't look the least bit sorry for it when she'd headed upstairs sometime ago.

They'd walked out into the yard just in time for Gracie, as her family called her, to tell Lilliane that she needed to be horsewhipped. He hadn't found out why yet that Gracie thought Lilliane needed to be treated to such a punishment, but he would before long. But like an idiot, he'd stepped between the two women just as Lilliane had drawn back her fist and socked him in the nose.

Before he could recover or drop to his knees and out of harm's way, Gracie had him down on his back and sat over his chest, drawing back to break more of his face before Cain pushed her off him. Gracie had thought that Shamus would retaliate against her sister and stepped in before he'd had a chance to explain. Christ, these people were very protective of each other. Shamus was glad he didn't have any sisters, and the next time Cain came into the room just to point and laugh, he was going to make sure they didn't have a brother either.

"How's your face?" Shamus looked over at Quinn as she sat next to him. One or two of them had come into the living room every ten minutes for the past hour and a half.

"It fucking hurts," he told her around the ice pack. "Where on earth did she learn to punch like that?"

"I taught her," Sin said as she came in with a toddler in her arms. She sat Conner on the floor before she sat down. "Pretty good at it too, huh? I taught all them some basics over the years. Some more than others. Lilliane, while not the best student, was certainly the most enthusiastic."

He'd learned from Devin that Sin had been in the Special Forces until a near fatal attempt on her life ended her career and her chances to have a child of her own. Then several months after being in the United States again, she'd lost a very good friend of hers in another attempt.

"Christ. If she wasn't the best student I'd hate to tangle with that one. Women don't fight fair." Shamus had meant it as a joke, but could see that it fell short. "I'm sorry."

"No, don't be." Quinn shifted on the seat before she continued. "I needed to learn to fight back. My ex-husband thought I made a wonderful punching bag and when I fought back, he left me alone."

"But not for good." Sin took up the story. "He thought he could get to her through someone I was very fond of. Tonya, my daughter, is named for Shipley, my buddy's mom. So I killed him back when he killed Shipley. I hate bullies."

When Alyssa and Grace entered the room, Shamus knew something was up. When Jazzie sat on the floor in front of the fireplace, Shamus looked around at them all. Simply beautiful and simply dangerous. He was sure there wasn't a woman here who wouldn't kick his ass and hand it to him on a platter.

"While any man would appreciate five of the loveliest women in the state of Ohio tending to him, you ladies just don't strike me as the domestic type. You're either up to something not good or you're up to no good. Which is it?"

"I told you he would freak out if we descended on him all at once," Sin said with a laugh. "I would if you all came into a room I was in and—oh wait, you have done it before."

"We need to talk to you about Lilliane," Alyssa finally said.

Chapter 10

Lilliane paced the floor to her room. Damn, damn, and double damn it. Of all the flights coming into that tiny airport, Gracie had to be landing at just that moment when she was getting ready to board.

Lilliane ignored the knock at her door like she had the dozen or so times someone had tried to talk to her before. She was pissed and she wasn't in the mood for a family meeting. She knew it was locked, so she continued her pacing.

She'd try again, that was all. Leaving meant the safety of everyone in this house and for as much as she dearly loved them, she thought she might shoot them all if she didn't leave soon. Someone clearing their throat had her jerking back around to the door.

"You do that well. Pacing, I mean. But did you know that you muttered when you did it? Very enlightening." Shamus moved from the door and jiggled a set of keys as he moved toward her. "Interesting things about locks on doors, the right set of keys can get you all kinds of information."

"Get out. I locked the door for a reason. Make sure you return it that way when you leave." She sat down on the edge of the bed. "I've had a really shitty day and you aren't making it any better."

"Gee, and I thought you'd tell me how sorry you were that you broke my nose." He moved into the room enough to shut the door. But as far as she knew, he was on the wrong side of it.

"Since you walked into my fist, I hardly see how I should be sorry for your stupidity. And as for you broken nose, I know it's not. It's too pretty to be anything but slightly bruised and you know it."

"You think my nose is pretty?"

Lilliane rolled her eyes at his question. "As I'm sure you know it is, I'm not dignifying that with an answer. You're much too cocky as it is." When he sat on the bed next to her, she hopped up and moved away. "What the hell do you think you're doing? I thought you wanted to slow things down. I'm sure this is putting the horse way out there before the cart again."

"About that—"

"No," Lilliane told him again when he stood. "I think you're right. You, you need to—what do you think you're doing now?"

She could see what he was doing; she was just having a hard time believing it. When he finished unbuttoning his shirt, she needed to swallow twice before she was reasonably sure her voice wouldn't squeak.

"I sleep better when I'm naked. I love the feel of cool sheets as they soothe my skin. Then there is the—"

"Cain is downstairs," she nearly screamed at him as she backed up again. Shamus' grin made her think of all kinds of things and none of them she'd repeat to him on threat of death.

"But I don't want to sleep with Cain. Besides, I'm pretty sure Alyssa would be pissed if I tried." He was less than a foot from her when he spoke again. "Let me touch you, Lilliane. Let me feel your warm skin against mine."

She did the only thing she could do under the circumstances. She bolted to the bathroom. And the door had one of those slidie locks, not the kind that needed a key. She slid the bolt home as he burst out laughing on the other side. She was terrified that if she'd stayed out there one more second with the man she'd be in those cool sheets with his naked body before he could ask her to join him. "This isn't going to go well with a door between us." She heard the humor in his voice. "What if I promised that I'd let you have your wicked way with me? Then would you let me open this door?"

Lilliane laid her head against the door. She had to curl her fingers into fists so that she didn't give in and do what he wanted. Hell, do what she wanted to do to that body of his.

"Why are you doing this? The sex couldn't have been all that good. I mean, I know that I must have been way below par to what you're used to."

"Below par? No, never that. Inexperienced, yes, but not below par. Open the door, please. I really want to talk to you."

She was shaking her head before she remembered he couldn't see her. Deciding to take a different route, she told him something her family didn't even know.

"He tried to have sex with me. My father, he tried to... It was right after Sin left. I was just coming out of the bathroom at home when he was suddenly there." She turned her back to the door and thought about that night. "He'd been drinking, him and mother. I'm not sure how drunk he was, but I could smell it on him."

"How old were you?"

Lilliane thought his voice sounded right behind her so she slid to the floor and curled her knees up under her chin. "I would have... Let me see, it was five days after Sin and I turned eighteen. I was going to take classes in the fall—about a month from then at the local college. I couldn't afford to live away from home even with the scholarship I'd won. Cain was already at the top of his class in med school and Quinn was married to Wickett and Grace had left the year before."

"Tell me about it."

He made is sound so easy. She took a deep breath and started at the beginning. "Mother loved her husband. They seemed to…I'm not sure if I ever saw them apart much. He even went to her yearly appointments with her. It wasn't until I was away for awhile and saw other families that I realized he didn't so much love her as he was controlling her. And she liked it." Lilliane laughed a hard, bitter laugh even to her ears. "He hated that he couldn't control Sin. God, he hated her for her temperament."

"And you, other than that night, how did he view you?"

"Willful. That's what he called me. Quinn was a doormat, Grace a bitch, and Jazzie was…she seemed to just let everything flow around her so he thought she was retarded. Not to be mean, though he was that. No, he actually thought she was mentally challenged. But me, I was willful." She smiled at a memory, wanting to steer clear of the attempted sex thing for now. "He told me that I couldn't play high school football. Actually, there were no rules about it so I worked with Jazzie and Sin to learn to be a kicker. Jazzie played soccer as a kid and Sin could simply kick. I was really good at it too. So in my junior year, I went out for the team. Sin was there, so was Jazzie when tryouts began. The first time I kicked the ball, I got it right through the uprights. That shut them up. Then everytime I scored, the coach would move me back five yards. I only bobbled it once, but still got it through. Then I was suddenly at the other team's forty yard line. You should have seen it. Every person in the school must have cut class early to watch."

She was seeing it, the field with the marching band marks on it, the uprights bright yellow in the afternoon light, the track field oval circling around the field like a brown smudge in the otherwise green oasis. She could even smell the air, hot and humid in the last of summer heat and sweat from hard work and fun.

"You can't stop there, love. Tell me the rest."

She grinned at his impatience. She'd forgotten he was still there. "Sin and the coach came across the field toward me. I thought he was coming to tell me that they'd found some ruling about the game and I couldn't play. That I gave a good try, but football, like my father had told me, was a sport for men—real men.

"But they didn't, did they? Please tell me that some-narrow minded teacher didn't burst your dream." He sounded like he was mad for her over something that had happened over twelve years ago.

"He told me that if I even got close that I'd be their reserve kicker. He said that he'd had a senior on the team that could kick, but since I was newer to the team and only a junior, he got to play first. But I would get a letter and that I would get to play some." Lilliane laughed. "After he walked away, Sin looked at me and said 'sink it.' That's all, just 'sink it,' and walked away."

"And did you?"

"She said it to me not like she thought that I could, but that I might not because I was on the team and there was no reason to try all that hard. She said it as though she believed me capable of doing it."

Lilliane hadn't thought of that before then. She knew that Sin had always believed in her; she just never realized how much.

"Lilliane?"

"So I did it. Nothing but air. Hang time was great and score, right through the middle."

Lilliane heard his laughter. It wasn't forced or fake-sounding. He sounded as though he'd really enjoyed her story. She suddenly wanted to see him, see him having a good chuckle at a younger her. She stood up and slid the lock open, not sure where he was, and opened the door cautiously. He was leaning with his back to the jamb with his legs stretched out in front of him.

"Come here, Lilliane." His voice was warm, low, and still had a bit of humor. When he opened his arms out for her, she moved forward slowly.

She dropped to her knees beside him and looked down, suddenly very nervous. "I'm not like my sisters. I have their temper but not their temperament. I run when I should fight and I'm incredibly shy. I want to be more like them, but I can't."

When Shamus lifted her head with his fingertips under her chin, she looked at his face. He didn't seem angry or disappointed but somewhat please with himself.

"Lilliane, I don't want you to be anything but what you want to be. And for the record, I think you're more like you sisters than you realize. You killed two gunmen with nothing more than your bravery when they would have killed you. You survived multiple gunshot wounds and you took down a seasoned cop with one blow." She grinned when he did.

"Yeah," she told him. "I'm all that and a bag of chips."

~~~

Shamus didn't think of himself as a fool often. He usually made a decision and stuck with it until the end. But he'd been one over his decision to keep Lilliane at arm's length. He wanted to rectify that now. Cupping the back of her head, he gently pulled her to his mouth.

He took her mouth softly, brushing his lips over hers. She was warm and responsive, her breath sweet and delicious against his mouth. When he pulled her closer, wanting to hold her, she put her hand on his bare chest and felt her heat sear into his skin. Reaching for her with his free hand, he guided her to his lap and never let go of her mouth. After a couple of small jabs with her elbows when he moved her, she was sitting across his lap facing him.

He wanted her. He wanted her beneath him, over him. He wanted to taste her, feel her surrounding his cock. Shamus wanted to bury his tongue deep inside of her pussy and drink from her while she came. He'd never wanted, never craved a woman like he did this one and it no longer scared the hell out of him.

Her fingers brushed over his bare nipple and he groaned against her mouth. When she pulled away, he stared at her through heavy-lidded eyes, his cock burning for release.

"I want to touch you. Feel your skin under my fingers, but I don't know…I don't want to hurt you."

He was hurting already, but didn't say that to her. Instead, he put his hands down to his thighs and tried to relax for her. He nodded to her. "Touch me, Lilliane. Touch me and feel what you want. Feel what you to do me with just your voice, your fingers, and your body."

He could see that she was unsure. For that matter, so was he. But he didn't lie to her. She couldn't hurt him, not like this.

She brushed her fingertips over his nipple again. He felt it tighten and pucker. When she ran her nail over the hardened peak, he couldn't help the groan and she jerked her hand back in alarm.

"You didn't hurt me. Christ, no. That felt good, better than good." He pulled her hands back to his chest and looked at her when his muscles quivered beneath her. "Touch away. But know this; I get to do the same to you when you're finished."

She nodded, but seemed distracted as she leaned in and ran her tongue over his nipple. His moan this time was a low grumble he felt to his toes and back again. She smiled at him and he knew that he was in big trouble. Really big trouble.

"Your skin is different than mine." He wanted to tell her that was what made her feel good to him, but was suddenly incapable of speech. She laved her hot tongue over his nipple again and he clenched his fists at his sides. No, he wasn't in trouble; he was surely a dead man.

As she moved her incredible mouth up his collar bone toward his neck, all sorts of hot and sexy thoughts and images ran through his mind. When she sank her teeth into his muscle where his neck met his shoulder, he said her name.

"Do you like that, Shamus? Because I do. I like the way you taste in my mouth. All warm and manly." She scooted her body up his lap and cradled his jean-covered erection between her thighs. "You're very hard."

"Yes," he hissed. "And getting harder."

Her giggle nearly sent him over the edge of control. "We can't have that now, can we?" she said with a bit of imp in her voice. "Can I give you some relief?"

Yes, his mind screamed at her. Relief in your mouth, your pussy, hell, your hand will work right now. When she rubbed the palm of her hand over his cock, he stayed her hand with his own.

"Baby, unless you want your lesson to end right now with me pounding you between those pretty thighs, I suggest you don't touch me there just yet. I'm ready to explode and doing it in my pants is not what I have in mind."

When he moved her hands to his thighs, he started to let go of the breath he hadn't been aware he'd been holding when she cupped him again. His blood was rushing through his brain so loud he couldn't hear; his skin was so hot he felt like he might combust at any second. The first button on his button-fly jeans gave way before he realized what she was doing. The third and fourth had him surging up to feel her touch him even if there was a brief touch of her fingers as she worked the buttons free.

"I don't... Help me get them down, Shamus. I don't know how to free you while you're sitting down."

The urgency in her voice caught him. He lifted his legs up to tilt his hips to a better angle and her body came flush with his. Taking her mouth, he was brutal, savage. He needed her now and wanted her to know it. Having her pull back made him snarl like a beast. His fingers tightened in her hair.

"Lilliane, now."

She didn't answer, but slid back from him and over his legs. He was about to follow her to go wherever she went when she wrapped her fingers around his cock. He nearly came. Before he could beg her to take him, beg her to please put him out of his misery, she spoke.

"I want you in my mouth. I want to taste you when you come. Let me, let me pull you into my mouth and take you."

His cock jerked hard. He watched her lower her head, watched her tongue reach out and lap at the heavy stream spilling from the tip. When she wrapped her lips around him, he moaned again, his fingers still tight in her hair flexed and gentled. She was going to kill him.

He moved her so that she could take him in her mouth while he could cup her breast. He wanted her naked flesh to fill his hand and even as he panted, his heart pounding, he tried to pull her shirt over her head. When she let go of his cock with a soft pop, he wanted to beg her to go back, but her clothes had to go.

When she stood to take her pants off, Shamus leaned in and buried his nose in her wet pussy.

"I want you. Right now, I want to fuck you. Hard, fast, and dirty until we both come." She hissed out her approval and he told her to go to the bed. "Bend over and brace your hands on the mattress. I'm going to fuck you from behind. Is that all right?"

She bent at the waist and opened her legs. Jerking his pants off the rest of the way as he stood up, he came up behind her and fisted his cock.

He couldn't speak. His need made him insane to be inside of her. Guiding just the engorged tip at her entrance, he leaned down just enough to nip her back. Then he stood up and slammed deep.

She screamed out her release. Her sheath rippled along his cock so tight he trembled behind her. Pulling out to the tip, he filled her again. His balls, already tight, ached in a way he'd never felt before. When he pulled out again, she was begging, moaning for more. Reaching between her legs, he pinched her clit and commanded her to come. When he thrust forward this time, her climax screamed from her mouth. He exploded inside of her.

Chapter 11

Nothing was going according to plan. Every time someone had one of her damned brats in their hands something or someone would spring them. First Alyssa, the money-grubbing whore, then Quinn and Sydney, and now this stupid thing with Lilliane had gone to shit. Maybe Ginny should concentrate on the men and leave the women alone until later.

Ginny liked that the mother hated the children too. It made it so much easier not to have to fight against such a wonderful ally. But the "poor me" shit was getting old. She'd have a talk with her when she saw her next. Tell her to grow a backbone or get the hell out of her way.

Guinevere's husband Roscoe had the right of it. Kill them all if they lost their usefulness and move on. Hell, he used to tell her he had six of them so what the hell did it mean to him if he lost one along the way? But that upstart son of his was the worst.

Always coming to the rescue just as the deal was about to be closed on another family death. Ginny was just glad she'd never had to part with her money much more than to set things up before some fuck-tard would come along and screw up her well-laid plans.

Like those two in Tennessee. They'd cost the most with their demands and had achieved the least of any of them. All they'd managed to do with their incredible stupidity was injure the teacher and kill a couple of rug rats. Oh, and let's not forget the cop that was suddenly in the picture. Another cop in the way as far as she was concerned was two too many. But this one, according to Guinevere, was smart, way too smart.

Fuck, as far as Ginny was concerned, all men were useless unless in the bedroom and any woman worth her salt should be able to lead him into anything she wanted if she was good enough or tight enough. She laughed. Oh yeah, she was going to lead this man on a merry chase.

Ginny looked over at the phone when it started to ring. She didn't answer it, but let it go on and on. After five rings the caller gave up. And she'd bet her last nickel that whoever it was was dialing it again. When the phone began to ring again less than a minute later she started laughing. People were so predictable. Still, she didn't bother. Instead, she sat at the little table Guinevere used as her makeup vanity.

Ginny didn't enjoy looking at the face that reflected back at her. She didn't like the harsh lines around her eyes or the deep ones around her mouth. She didn't like thinking about the passing of years and she didn't like the thought of dying. Picking up one of the twenty or so brushes there she played with some of the fine powders without real interest until a movement out of the corner of her eye had her looking into the furious stare of the woman behind her. Without bothering to turn she spoke to Guinevere. "Did you speak to your son? I'm not sure how much longer we can continue to live like this. It was all right when Roscoe was here to distract me, but now that it's just you..." Ginny let the threat go unfinished. She loved rubbing in her face that Roscoe preferred her over his own wife when he needed to be fucked. A small shiver danced down her spine when she thought of him and his hard sex.

"He said that this place is plenty big enough. He said that if I wanted any more increases in the size of my house then I should think about going out and getting a job." Guinevere sat on the side of the bed as she kicked off her shoes. "That bitch has him on a tight leash. He couldn't even come with me to the movies because he'd had plans with his wife. Tell me, who picks their wife over their own dear mother?"

"This is not acceptable Guinevere. Maybe we should demand he do something. We need money—"

"I can't very well demand we need more money so that we can kill his family off, now can I?

Ginny didn't like the way Guinevere was beginning to show signs of rebellion. She didn't like the fact that she was beginning to show she was getting stronger too.

Roscoe had been able to keep his wife in line with just a word. She wondered if he had always worked that way or if he'd needed to discipline his wife a bit at first to get her to understand who was in charge. She'd come later in their lives. She didn't know for sure, but decided that she needed to take a better position from now on.

Guinevere was suddenly on the floor with her hand covering her mouth. "You'll do well not to use that tone with me. I'm not one of your daughters to push around like a mindless idiot."

Guinevere didn't move. There were no tears, not even a drop of blood, but Ginny felt she'd made her point. If the brief glint of defiance gave her pause, Ginny would bet her life Guinevere wasn't aware of it.

"Tomorrow we'll start planning for the attack on that cop, the one the teacher has a crush on. After we get rid of him, then we'll go back to her. She doesn't have the backbone to stand up like that army dyke does."

Sydney, her name was. Ginny hated that daughter almost as much as she hated Cain. The girl was smart, too smart for her own good, and too fucking strong to just think that a few bullets to her body would stop her. No, it would take more than that to bring that bitch down. Damn, Ginny would be glad when this whole thing was over.

Ginny watched Guinevere move out of the room. Soon, she would have to go as well. Ginny decided she was going to have Cain between her legs if it was the last thing she did. Or for that matter, the last thing he did.

With a maniacal laugh Ginny got up to dress. She'd been sitting around this dump long enough. It was high time she got out and saw a little of the night life.

~~~

"She wants a bigger house," Cain said to his wife as soon as they'd both put Connor to bed and gone back to the living room.

Cain watched Alyssa remove her shoes and slide her legs up under her as she sat down on the couch. He realized he'd gotten slightly distracted when she snapped her fingers in front of his face.

Her laughter made his cock twitch hard in his pants. "Come here and hold me. I've had a really crappy day."

She slid along the dark brown leather and onto his lap. He loved just holding her almost as much as he enjoyed making love with her.

"What did she say she needed a bigger house for?" He looked at her, confused. "Focus, Cain. Your mother? House? Bigger?"

He cupped Alyssa's breast in his hand "Just thinking of your nipple in my mouth makes me bigger. Harder too, painfully so." He lifted her up enough to settle her across his lap so that she faced him. "Oh yes. This is better, much better. Now where was I? Oh, I know, here."

Her nipple hardened in his mouth. Even through the silk of her blouse she had on and the tiny bit of lace, he could almost taste her. Running his fingers up and under the silk he rubbed his thumb under her bra and right over the full, lush breast. Both their moans seemed to bounce around them in the large room.

"Cain, we were going to cuddle. You said—" Her breath left her throat audibly when he freed her and suckled hard on just the tip. When she rocked her hips, cupping her pussy around his cloth-covered erection, he nearly cried out.

"Baby, I want you to take me like this. Ride me slowly and deep while I feast on these luscious breasts."

Her hands went to the clasp on his pants and pulled it free. He was glad he'd opted for suspenders today when she opened his fly and cupped him through his briefs.

"Cain, help me. Please? I can't get your—" He slid forward on the couch slightly and leaned back. Her hiss of approval was nearly enough to have him come when she suddenly freed him.

His cock ached. Not only that, but when he glanced down at her small hands wrapped around him, his eyes rolled to the back of his head. When she rose to her knees over him and lifted her skirt up Cain whimpered.

"How long have you been walking around pantiless?" His voice croaked with need.

"Since before we took Connor to his bed. I've been wet for you a lot longer, though. All day as a matter of fact."

She'd planned this, his mind screamed. Hot damn, she wanted this too. Cain wrapped his hands into her hair and pulled her mouth just to his and whispered to her. "What would you have done if I didn't want to make love tonight?" Her grin was wicked, so much so that he couldn't help but feel his cock leak more. "Alyssa?"

"Then I would have used something from the big box of toys that came for us in the mail today. Something in there would have been able to do the trick, I'm sure."

It took him several seconds for his lust-filled mind to register what she'd said. When it finally made it through his blood-starved brain to his thought process, he nearly knocked them both to the floor, tripping over the coffee table trying to stand.

"Where are you going?" she giggled. "The box is still in your office."

The detour to his office almost resulted in a fatal accident involving a priceless vase on a stand and a flower pot. Finally he was pressing her between his hips and a wall while he fumbled with the knob. The door wasn't cooperating and he had to take possession of her mouth again to keep her from laughing at him. That shut her up but made him needier.

They ripped the box open and dumped the contents onto his desk as they settled in his desk chair. Alyssa sat in his lap again only this time, her back was to his chest. Her skirt was still bunched around her waist with her trimmed pussy showing. When they both grabbed for the vibrating anal dildo, Cain knew what he wanted.

"Stand up and lean over for me." The hunger in her eyes was so primal he nearly came looking at her.

Without a word, she stood up and braced her palms on the large oak desk. When she opened her stance Cain moaned at what she was showing him.

It only took him a second to peel off the sterile wrapper and insert the batteries. Reaching into his desk drawer, he pulled out a handful of alcohol wipes and tore two of them open. He wiped down the toy even as several of the wipes hit the floor. The bright blue tiny cock came alive when he turned the button. Alyssa moaned and rocked her hips back toward him.

"You like the sound?" She nodded. "Me too. It reminds me what I'm going to do to you, with you."

Leaning forward, Cain jabbed his tongue into her pussy from behind. He drank from her this way, feasting on her cream as she flooded his mouth. He rubbed the dildo over her back entrance even as he pushed the finger of his free hand deep into her quivering sheath.

Her climax was powerful and loud. And while she filled his mouth with her juices Cain pushed the thin latex toy past her tight muscles.

"Cain. Oh my God, Cain, yes," she cried out.

He knew he hadn't hurt her, much anyway. They'd been working her ass for weeks now, preparing her for his cock. Tonight all his patience had snapped with her sobs. Standing, Cain fisted his cock and teased her clit with it as he worked the small toy in and out of her tightness.

Every noise she made, every whimper, every groan had his balls tightening more. He continued to tease her clit with his cock as she tried over and over to rock back and take more of him in her. As soon as he pulled the tiny cock out of her ass then began to move it back and forth inside of her again, he slammed his cock into her dripping pussy to the hilt.

"Christ," he breathed. "You're tight and, baby, I can feel the dildo. Its vibrations are running up and down my cock like it's actually touching me."

He pulled his cock out with every inward motion of the toy. When he filled her again, the toy would only work at the tight ring at her dark hole until he started again. His cock was soaked as were his balls from her juices. When his climax grabbed him it was so unexpected that he cried out his release as he continued to rock into her hard. Her own release nearly had him begging her to stop she was milking him so tightly.

When he dropped back into the chair he brought Alyssa with him. He'd already turned off his new favorite toy and laid it on the wood of the desk. He knew it would leave a mark and actually looked forward to seeing the stain there to remember what they'd done. Cuddling his wife in his arms, he held her to him as both their breathing returned to normal.

"So," she said with a huge yawn, "you were saying something about your mother."

Cain couldn't help it, he burst out laughing with a light squeeze to her. He stood her up, gathered their unused purchases, and tossed them back in the box along with the used one. With a shoulder to her belly he hefted her up and over him and took her to their room.

He smiled when he saw their clothes on the couch and floor. The staff would be giggling tomorrow, he thought, and realized he didn't care. He was a man who dearly loved his wife and didn't care who knew it.

Chapter 12

"This is the merger deal that you talked about. Most of the workers have decided to stay on, a few took the early retirement option we put in place, and even fewer decided to quit. I think you should be pleased."

Alyssa looked over the papers her brother handed her as they sat at the small conference table in her office. He had even attached a sheet with the list of names she'd requested and he'd put what they had decided to do beside each name in his neat handwriting.

"This is great, Nathan. You've closed the deal two months ahead of schedule and saved the company a great deal of money. Thanks." She watched him flush. She wondered if he'd get used to people complementing him and hoped so. He'd proven himself a great asset to her firm and someone she had come to rely on.

In the year since she'd hired him he'd already made great progress. She knew he was attending his AA meetings regularly. She and Cain had even gone with him a few times when he'd asked. She knew he struggled, they both did. But hopefully they'd be able to make it work for them.

Nathan was technically not her brother, but her half brother. Their mother, Shannon Howard, had been married to her father when he'd been conceived. Alyssa was her father's only child even though there were three children born to her mother. Their other brother, half to them both, was Robert, but he and their mother had been killed last year.

"It wasn't just me," he told her proudly. "It was the people you gave me to work with. They did most of the major leg work. And that lady...Lana, she can certainly make a computer work for her."

Alyssa didn't bother telling him that his team had come to her about his leadership skills. He wouldn't believe her and he'd be embarrassed again. Alyssa decided to have him work on the next project she had on her desk and reached for it.

"This is something I need help on too." She frowned when she read the name on the folder and looked at him. "This guy has been stalling for over four months on moving out of the building we purchased from him six months ago. He had the normal sixty days, but now it's putting us behind on revamping the building for something else."

Nathan opened the file. "What's his excuse? It says here that..." He looked at her. "This is Uncle Samuel's building."

She nodded then stopped. "Sort of. When he died all his holdings in this venture went to his partner, Douglass Kennedy. Neither man seemed to have much business sense, but it seemed the business made some money despite their skills, or lack of them really. If you'd rather not do it, Nathan, I understand. I have plenty of other projects I can use your help with."

He didn't say anything for several minutes and she watched him read over the contents of the folder. After a few minutes more she returned to her own desk and started working on the prospectus she had been involved with when he came in. His clearing his throat had her looking up at him after almost an hour.

"Sorry about that. I got distracted. This company could make you some serious money if you did it right. There is everything you need to… I'm sorry. What did you want me to do with it?"

She got up, sat in the chair opposite his, and took the file. She opened it and looked at the papers.

The company manufactured tin toys. They made reproductions of the ones in an antique book she'd seen in her father's study as a child. But poor management, lack of funds, and a general exasperation of other things had put them in the red deep and they'd never been able to recover again.

"Tell me what you see. I mean, besides the normal bad business sense. What do you see that the others didn't that says it's a worthy business?"

"Not bad business sense but bad timing. Look." He pulled the file to him again and took out several sheets of paper. "They have all the equipment to manufacture; most of it is less than five years old. What they lack is orders to get rid of the merchandise they have. If they did that they'd have the capital to make more product to pay their bills to buy more material to make… Well, you get it," he said with a flush.

She grinned and looked at the inventory hard. He was right. They did have a great deal of finished product. Millions of dollars worth, as a matter of fact. Even the boxes to ship it in were paid for and already at the plant.

"I don't know anything about selling off toys," she told him. "And I would imagine neither did the owner. We'd have to…I don't suppose you could close this deal and make this work for the employees, could you? It would certainly be much better than closing it down and having to let go all those employees."

"There was this man…he wasn't an addict like me, but a dad of—anyway. His son tried to hang himself one night and I sort of kept him from strangling to death. The dad told me that he'd always owe me. He owns a few stores. I won't ask him to take the toys, but I will ask him to teach me how to market them."

Alyssa closed the file and handed it to him. She wouldn't ask him about saving someone or how he "sort of" did it. She'd learned that he wouldn't share until he was ready.

"It's yours. Keep me posted and, if you need Drew, just remember to keep track of his hours. I don't need accounting on my butt again about billable hours." She sat back in the chair. "Great job, Nathan. I'm really glad you came to work for Cain and me."

He flushed again.

Jazzie came in the door before he could speak, banging the door open and coming in the room like a small tornado or a major earthquake. She smiled at Nathan. "Hello, handsome. You're taking me to lunch. I want to try out that new place on Tenth Avenue. And I hate eating alone."

"I can't have lunch with you again, Miss Waite. Besides, the last time we ate together you wouldn't stop telling people I was your lover." Nathan stood, nodded to Alyssa, and practically ran to the door and left.

"He's always doing that. Running away from me like I've got something. It could give a girl a complex. Doesn't he know that we're related and he's supposed to find me charming and fun?"

Alyssa laughed. "Come on, I'll have lunch with you. But no telling anyone we're lovers. Cain gets nervous when you do that."

Jazzie laughed hard and loud. "Why do you think I do it?"

~~~

Shamus was drinking his second cup of coffee when Lilliane came down. He hid his smile behind his cup when she blushed. Thankfully, Cain didn't seem to notice as he was playing with his son.

She began fussing with the tea pot on the stove so Shamus got up and brushed against her on the way to the sink. Her breath seemed to catch and he nearly leaned in and nipped at her exposed neck. The only thing that kept him from doing it was Cain speaking to him.

"I got the keys to the house for you. Alyssa called in a service and had it cleaned top to bottom. She wasn't sure of your cooking abilities so she had foodstuffs of the general nature brought in and set in the kitchen pantry. The fridge is stocked as well."

"You're moving?" Lilliane asked. "I wasn't aware you planned to…I guess I never realized you weren't staying here."

"I've been hoteling it. But I have some things I need to make sure your protected so Cain offered me his house to stay in." He wanted to ask her to come with him, but knew she would refuse.

Last night after they'd cuddled up in her bed she told him her brother was extremely protective of them. She said that she wouldn't disrespect him, especially in his house, by having an affair openly with someone.

Shamus wanted to deny that what they had wasn't simply an affair, but didn't. To be honest, he wasn't sure what they had going on. He liked her, the sex was great, but after this was over, he knew they'd be going their separate ways—him back to New York or Tennessee and her to wherever.

The phone ringing startled him and when the cook answered Cain stood and held Connor over his head. He started to reach for the phone, probably thinking it would be for him, when she said it was for Miss. Lilliane. Lilliane told her to send it to the office.

Cain handed his son to Shamus as he started pulling on his jacket to leave for work. He picked up his case and put his hand on the door knob.

"So, you think you'll be able to find who supplied the guns to those men with all that fancy equipment?"

Shamus nodded. "Yes. If not, then it won't be from lack of trying. I'm trying my best to keep your sister safe, Cain."

"I know that." Cain opened the door. "By the way, you might want to tell Lilly Pad to put some lotion on the burns at her neck. It makes the whisker burns less red. Or, of course, you could just shave before going to bed." And with that he slipped out the door.

Shamus sat there for a full minute, Connor held just above the high chair he was about to set him in, before he threw back his head and laughed. He knew. Cain knew they were lovers. Asking the cook if she could keep an eye on the little boy he went to find Lilliane. If her brother knew they were sleeping together, maybe she could move in with him. His cock jumped at the thought. He found her in the big office still on the phone.

"Yes. I'm sure… No, I can get there," she told the person on the phone. "All right, I'll see you there."

As she hung up Shamus pulled her from the chair and into his arms. Touching her seemed as vital to him as breathing. And when she lifted her face up to look at him, tasting her seemed a good idea as well. The kiss felt right.

"Where do you think you're going?" he asked her when they finally came up for air. "Because I'm thinking we should go back up to the bed and make love for a couple of hours."

"I can't," she told him as she pulled away. "I have to…I'm going to go to the Montessori School to sub. I think."

When she suddenly sat back down and put her head between her knees Shamus became alarmed. He rubbed her back when she started breathing in her nose and out her mouth.

"They need someone to teach a sixth grade class and they want me to do it. They had someone lined up and she suddenly quit." She looked up at him with tears in his eyes. "I don't know if I can do this."

He wanted to tell her she wasn't going to, but knew that this would be a way for her to feel better about herself and teaching. Instead, he asked her about the job.

"They said it would only be for a couple of days. Alyssa told them to call me. Mrs. Jolly, the principal, said that she and Alyssa's husband worked on a project together."

"Would you mind if I called Alyssa and asked?" Lilliane shook her head. So after a few minutes speaking with Alyssa, it was confirmed that she had recommended her for the job and she'd given her the number to reach her.

Now what? He knew she wanted to do this. He knew she needed to do this. She needed to walk into the classroom and teach those kids and not fall apart. He smiled when he thought of what Sin would do. "Yeah, I guess you're right." She looked up at him. "I mean, someone who's afraid of her own shadow and who would fall apart at the first issue can't be teaching a bunch of sixth graders math and social studies."

"I'm not afraid of my... How dare you say something... I'll show you scared." She stood up and march to the door. "I can teach anything I want to anyone. And you, Mr. Big Stupid Policeman, are to stay away from me."

When the door slammed, he stood up and went to the door. One of his men was standing there looking up the stairs. When Shamus stood beside him, Tim looked at him.

"She said I was taking her to school." Tim looked back up the stairs again when another door slammed. "She ain't left the house in weeks. Now she is."

"So it would seem. Are you okay to take her?" Tim started to shake his head before Shamus finished. "Why not?"

"She ain't left the house, so I didn't drive. My wife...she needed the car and I didn't think she'd be leaving."

Shamus smiled. He was going to be with her anyway.

~~~

The school was set back on a piece of property, well away from the city limits. The grounds, what they could see of them, were plush and well maintained. The gate in the front they were sitting at was high, steel, and also well guarded.

"Thank you for your patience, Detective McKee," the disembodied voice said through the speaker. "Captain Grant said that you would show us your driver's license and if you match the picture she sent us, we'll allow you to come in with Miss Waite."

After holding up his license the large gate slowly opened. Shamus could see the guard house then. It was a steel cage with, he'd bet, bullet proof glass around it. The man in the fortified shed nodded once and didn't have any bones about showing that he was armed. Shamus turned to Lilliane.

"You'll certainly be safe in here all day. I doubt they'd let the President in without as much fuss as they did me."

"I think it's great. I'd feel safe sending my children here. It may be prisonlike to some, but to me it's very calming." She took a deep breath before continuing. "I guess I was a lot more scared than I thought."

Shamus didn't say anything. He couldn't. All he could think about was what she'd said. Her child. He suddenly had visions of her swollen with his child. Round and full, her belly would be a great source of pride for him. He shook his head at the dream. Women like Lilliane Waite did not marry poor men like him. They married rich men, princes and actors. He parked in a visitor parking place and turned to her again.

"Someone will be back to get you at three o'clock. Don't leave the premises without one of us. I'm sure you'll be safe in here provided that no one on the staff is out for your blood, but I want you to be very careful. Do you have your cell phone?"

She nodded. "You won't be coming back to get me? I thought...I'll be fine. Just send that nice man who was—"

"Lilliane." He grabbed her arm before she could slide out of his vehicle. "We can continue to see each other, but we both know that this won't work."

She jerked her arm free and got out of the car. "Of course. I don't want you to come back, Mr. McKee. And I think you're right. I'll talk to Alyssa when I get home tonight and we'll see about getting you back to where you belong. Just let her or Cain know where that is and I'll see to it."

She slammed the door and hurried to the building before he could get his belt off to follow her. Damn it, he'd handled that wrong, he thought. Before he could change his mind and follow her inside—which he was reasonably sure he wouldn't be able to—he started his engine and left the grounds.

He was nearly home when he realized he was being followed.

Chapter 13

Lilliane was eating lunch when her phone vibrated in her pocket. She pulled it out, looked at the caller ID, and smiled. Alyssa had called twice now. Once, she left a message; the second time, a text. She loved the woman dearly.

"You're worried for nothing, you know. I'm doing just fine and dandy now," Lilliane said as a greeting. "The students are very well behaved and they seem to be extremely smart."

"They are. They have to be rated high on the tests they take at an early age to be admitted. They have a waiting list a mile long to get in there. I already have Connor on it."

Lilliane looked up when one of the other teachers asked to sit with her. She nodded. "I would bet you'd have no problem getting him in if you worked at it. I'm having fun. I didn't...I wasn't sure..."

When she didn't...couldn't finish, Alyssa seemed to understand. "Shamus said you'd been ready to give up teaching. I had hoped that this would sort of jump start you back into the game. You love it too much to give it up because of somebody's stupidity."

"I know." Lilliane looked at the man sitting with her and smiled. "I guess that'll never work out. I want to talk to you about his contract when I get home. It needs to end. And I was wondering if I could stay a bit longer before I decide what to do for myself?"

"Of course. You're welcome to stay here for as long as you want, honey. And as for things working out, don't worry about that part. I'll take care of it right now. Just let this other thing get over with then we'll go from there."

After they hung up Lilliane decided that she was going to tell them to let Shamus go back to wherever. The longer he stayed, the harder it was going to be on her. She was already half in love with the man and she'd not known him all that long.

"You must be the substitute teacher for Caroline. She had a wedding to go to in California tomorrow. I'm Denver Garner and I teach Phys Ed."

"Lilliane Waite. Yes, the children told me why I was here." She opened her sandwich and started to put the hamburger together. "I'm really impressed with the overall school. How long has it been here?"

She wanted to pull her sweater on. The man kept staring at her breasts and she had the feeling he had her completely naked in his mind already. She tried to hunch over to make her large breasts seem smaller, but his short laugh made her realize he knew what she was doing.

"Ten years. I think it was built from some endowment program. Some old rich guy built it. Howard somebody... I think he wanted to make sure that kids got a good education in a safe place. I don't care. It pays well and the kids are too rich to care if they get an education or not."

It took Lilliane a few seconds to realize what he'd said. Howard? She started to wonder if it was Alyssa's father and knew suddenly that it was. She wanted to laugh, but didn't. The pervert across from her wouldn't understand and besides, she was beginning to feel like she needed a shower—hot with lots of bleach. She hurried through her meal and got up to leave. He stopped her with a hand on her wrist.

"Hey, why don't you and I hook up after this? There's plenty of room to do the nasty in the office they gave me. Could be a great way to get to know each other." He wiggled his brows at her and she wanted to smash her tray over his head. Before she could do anything so stupid another teacher came to her rescue.

"Let her go, Garner. She's too nice for your sleaze." When he didn't, the other teacher stepped closer and he finally let her go. "See that you leave her alone. You have enough to worry about without a sexual harassment issue to compound things too."

Lilliane walked away with the woman. She didn't take a deep breath until they had disposed of their trays and were out of the lunch room. The woman smiled at her.

"I'm Marion Riddle. I'm the human resources manager. I was wondering if you'd come to my office for a few minutes? There are a few hundred pages of background checks I would like you to sign off on."

Lilliane nodded. "I have a few minutes. I still have this morning's tests to finish grading. But sure." She wanted to ask about Denver, but Marion started telling her as soon as her door shut.

"He's been in trouble outside the school. But nothing as yet that we can pin on him in here. He's been very...discreet, I guess you could say."

"What kind of stuff outside the school, if you don't mind my asking? I know...I realize that I'm new, but I've had some issues myself that I don't know if you're aware of." Lilliane was pretty sure they all knew but didn't know how much.

"Yes, when I talked with Mrs. Waite this morning she told me what you'd been through. She said that you were a hell of a teacher and just needed to have something to get you motivated again to teach. The thing with Garner is petty stuff, driving under the influence and a couple of domestic calls. He's married, by the way. I was...I'll be honest with you, Miss Waite. I want to keep you here. The teacher you're replacing isn't returning. She has a better offer out west and she's taking it. What would I have to do to get you to stay on?"

Lilliane sat back on the chair. She was stunned. A job, here? It was better than she could hope for. She looked up as a thought occurred to her. "This job, is it because my family asked you to give it to me? Because, if it is, I'm going to have to turn you down. I am a good teacher, but I want a job on my merits, not because my family is a bunch of busy-bodies that need to mind their own business."

Marion laughed. "No, but I'm impressed. I didn't think you were the kick ass and take names later sort of person. Yes, you'll do fine here. No, I'm offering you this job because of the references we got from the school you were at in Tennessee. The HR manager and the teachers couldn't say enough great things about you. Even before the shooting you were their hero it seems."

Lilliane flushed. "I don't know what you mean. I was just a teacher. I enjoyed it, but I'm not sure that I'm staying here. I was thinking of returning to Nashville. I liked it there."

Marion handed her a file. "This is the contract that Mrs. Jolly and I worked up for you. Salary information and benefits are all in there as well as anything else we could think of to keep you. Also, I'd like for you to keep this to yourself until you decide. The other teachers aren't aware of Caroline leaving yet."

Lilliane took the file and stood when Marion did. She was back in her classroom when the children came tumbling in after recess. The next three hours seemed to fly by. Several times she wanted to pull the file out that Marion had given her and look it over, but didn't want any of the children to know. She could look it over just as easily when she got home, she kept telling herself. When she was finishing up the last of the test papers there was a knock at the door.

She looked up to see one of the men from the house standing there. He didn't look all that happy either. She decided that she wasn't disappointed that it wasn't Shamus there, but happy. It would be better for everyone if he was let go to do whatever it was he wanted. Before she…well, just before she decided.

Ronnie Hayes was the policeman that came to get her. The school was willing to give a select few badges to get in through the gate, but they were not willing to give everyone one. She would just have to decide who was coming and going for her.

"Detective McKee said you were to go to your brother's, is that all right, ma'am?" She looked over at Ronnie. "I can take you most anywhere you wanna go, but I can't let you go all by your lonesome."

She wondered if his good ol' boy routine made women trust him more. He was a huge man; not fat, but muscled. She could see why he'd been picked. Lilliane started to tell him that was fine, but changed her mind.

"Can you take me to my sister-in-law's office? I haven't been there but once or twice so I don't know the way."

"Sure can," he told her with a smile. "You just go on ahead and give her a call and let her know you're a'coming and I'll get you there in a jiffy."

A "jiffy" turned out to be ten minutes and Alyssa was thrilled to have her come by. She was going to a meeting and wanted to have some company. Cain apparently had bailed on her.

"He hates these things as much as I do. But the difference is I have to go. He can pretend that he has something at the hospital. Turd."

The meeting turned out to be an awards dinner. Lilliane wasn't sure she wanted to go along either, but Alyssa said it was going to be boring and she wanted someone she could talk to. It was an awards thing for community services and she didn't know that many of the people there.

They arrived back at the house at nearly nine. Shamus was waiting on the front steps of the mansion when they arrived and he looked pissed off.

"I would have thought he'd be much happier with me than he looks." Lilliane looked at Alyssa before she continued. "You said he was free of the contract, right?"

"Yes. I called his boss back in Nashville and assured them he'd done a wonderful job, but we didn't want to take up any more of the man's time. He assured me that there would be no repercussions on Shamus' part and that the position he'd been working for was still his."

Before she could step from the vehicle he was pulling her along to his. She tried to pull away, but he wouldn't let go. Finally, she stopped moving. He'd either have to let her go or talk to her. He did neither.

Before she knew it, she was flipped over his shoulder with her head bobbing along his lower back. She'd never been so pissed or humiliated in her life.

"Put me down, you overgrown ox. I'm not going anywhere with you. As a matter of fact, why aren't you speeding down the highway toward—oof!" He dropped her on the passenger seat. "What do you think you're doing?"

"I'm trying my best not to bend you over my knee and bust your ass. I would suggest that you keep your mouth shut until we get to the house. Otherwise, I might be tempted to gag you." When she opened her mouth he simply raised a brow at her. She wasn't sure what the threat meant, but she closed her mouth with a snap.

She never said a word to him on the trip to Cain's old house. Which was easy since he didn't speak to her either. She did hear his cell phone ring twice, but he never once pulled it out. She realized then that she didn't have her purse or bag and she had school in the morning. When she pulled out her cell phone from her pocket he snatched it from her and threw it to the back seat.

As soon as the car stopped she threw open the door and unsnapped the seatbelt in one smooth move. While he was striding to the door she was making her way back the way they'd come. She was about ten feet away when she heard him shout at her. She took off running as soon as he did.

She didn't get far. Her leg was healed but still weak. But she didn't go as easy as she did at Cain's house. When he tried to use the same move on her, tossing her over his shoulder, she fought back. A fist to the belly had him growl at her and when he tried to take her again she fought like her life depended on it. Which, she supposed, it sort of did.

Before she could get more than a foot from him, he'd wrestled her to the ground and held her there with his body. She fought, but he was simply too big for her and she'd worn herself out.

"If you're finished now, we can go into the house and have a conversation. But if not…well, we can certainly have it here." She glared up at him. "Or, if you want, I can hold you here until you fall asleep then take you inside. Any way you look at it, I'm going to get my way."

"I hate you." He grinned when she said that. "I really do. I told Alyssa to let you out of the contract. What do you want now, to kidnap me?"

"No. And I didn't ask you to let me out of the contract. I said when this is over we'll go our separate ways. How did you get that in your mind that I wanted to be let go?"

She didn't answer because she wasn't sure. She wanted him to stay; she wanted him to want to stay. Now she didn't know what he wanted. She said as much to him.

"I want this to be finished. I want you and your family safe. I can't very well do that two states away." She felt his cock when he moved. "I also wanted to be with you again. If you don't want to sleep with me, that's fine, but...well, no it's not fine. I want you. As for leaving...I think we both know that you're well out of my league."

Before she could ask what the hell that meant he was standing up. She nearly pulled him back down on top of her when she could see his erection pressing against his jeans.

"Lilliane, you keep looking at me like that and we're never going to get our conversation started until after I'm buried deep inside of you. Come on," he said as he held out his hand for her to take. "Let's go inside. I have something I want you to see."

She took his hand and was thrilled that he didn't let it go when she was upright. She watched as he pulled out keys and unlocked the big house. She didn't know why she assumed that he was staying in the smaller house on the property.

Cain had purchased this land with the two separate residences on it before he'd met Alyssa. Devin Grant, his friend since Cain had been a kid, had sold it to him cheap because he and his wife no longer used it. It had six bedrooms and a nice two-bedroom cottage out back.

They were barely in the door when he pulled her to him. His mouth was hot as it pressed against hers. Before she could manage to touch him he was dragging her to the living room. She dug in her heels when he started for the stairs. She wanted him this time, not the other way around.

"I want you. I don't think I can ever get—"

"Are we alone here?" she asked, cutting him off. He nodded. "Good."

She walked to him and watched his eyes darken. "Lilliane, what are you going to do to me?"

She had no idea, but she was going to do something. She reached up and began unbuttoning his shirt. When he reached out to do the same to hers, she took a step back. This was her time.

"Don't touch me. I want to explore you, touch you, and I don't want you to distract me. Will you trust me, please?"

"Yes. I can't…I'll try is all I can do. I've never wanted a woman like I do you. Never wanted to—" She pressed her hand over his mouth.

"Be quiet. Just be quiet." She started working the small buttons through the holes again. "Every time we've had sex it's been sort of fast. Not that it wasn't great, but I want to see you. I want to…I want to take you."

His deep groan had her look up at his face. At his nod she finished his shirt but left it on him. Working her hands inside of it and toward his back, she felt his muscles ripple beneath her fingertips. Leaning in, she kissed the indentation between his breasts. Walking around him, she ran her finger along his shoulder until she was standing behind him.

Chapter 14

Shamus closed his eyes when she reached her hands up along his neck. He felt his entire body clench in anticipation of what she was going to do next. She started to peel his shirt off him; he moaned when she pressed kisses along his spine as she exposed it.

She was taking her time and trying to kill him, he realized. She took the shirt completely off and was folding it neatly when she stepped back in front of him. She seemed mesmerized by him and it made him stand still for her.

"You're very beautiful. Your muscles are so well defined it makes me want to touch each one of them to see if it feels as good to me as it looks."

He wanted to tell her to touch him, but he also found he wanted to beg her not to. When she stepped back to him she did touch him. Her fingers trailed a path along the muscles in his chest then down along the waistband of his jeans. He couldn't control the muscles when they jumped, nor the growl of approval that spilled from his mouth. When she paused at the snap of his jeans she looked up at him.

"You can't touch me, Shamus. Not at all. I want to have my way with you, please. If you can't allow me this then we can do this your way."

His way. His way was to take her hard and fast right now. His way would be to throw her over his shoulder, take her to the bedroom, and ravish her. But he could see the need in her eyes, not of simply lust, but to please him.

"Touch me, Lilliane. Do what you will to me. I'll not distract you...as much as I can. Take what you need from me."

Nodding, she leaned in and touched her tongue to his nipple. The feel of it puckering tight made him ache to have her. Her small teeth nipped at him and he nearly reached for her, only to drop his hands back to his sides before she could speak. Warm hands rested at his waist and her breath tickled the hair on his chest. He watched her every move, her every touch.

By the time she unsnapped his pants he was breathing hard. His cock hurt to be free and his balls felt like they were rising to his throat. Still, he didn't touch her, didn't speak any words.

"Your skin is so hot. And you taste...you taste like you. I know that sounds silly, but I would think this is just how you'd taste if I hadn't tasted you before." Her breath on his belly had him groan again. "I love the noises you make, the way you tell me without words how much you're enjoying this."

His tongue was too thick, his throat too dry. When she dropped to her knees before him he nearly swayed on his feet. Shamus watched as she struggled with the zipper, his cock pressing hard against it and making it near impossible for it to slide down smoothly. When she finally got it to pull he sighed heavily the relief of pressure felt wonderful. Then he couldn't breathe.

She rubbed her cheek along his cloth-covered cock. Her eyes closed, the look of rapture evident on her face. The temptation to hold her there, to guide her mouth to him, was overwhelming and he clenched his fists to keep from touching her.

"Baby. Baby, please. I need you." Even to his own ears he sounded desperate, his voice low and heavy. "I'm not going to last much longer."

Lilliane pulled away and he whimpered. With her hands at his hips she smiled up at him and began to pull his pants down, careful of his cock still hard against the material.

She touched him everywhere. His hips, his abdomen. She touched his inner thigh and his knee. Her fingers brushed against his balls and the curve of his ass. By the time she was pulling his pants off his feet he was panting, his heart pounding.

But she wasn't finished with him yet. She nipped along his cock, still within his boxer briefs. Her teeth grazed along him, wetting his shorts with her saliva and making him beg her to please let him touch her. He was nearly at his breaking point when she pulled the briefs down and took him into her mouth.

Never had a climax hit him so hard. His balls, already tight against his body, seemed to tighten incredibly more as he filled her mouth. His shout of completion went on as long as he jettisoned into her hot mouth. When her hand came up and cupped him he grabbed her hair and held on as he began to rock into her mouth, fucking her hard and not able to stop.

When he pulled back, his body spent, he staggered to the couch behind him and fell, glad that it was there. She stood then and he felt his cock jerk. He wanted her still. Needed her.

"Come here. Come here and let me taste you." She walked slowly forward, pulling her blouse off as she did. When she unzipped her skirt and let it fall he stopped her. "That's enough. I want to take you like this."

Her heels were thin and sharp, adding three inches to her height. The black patent leather that crossed over her foot met the other side with a small heart of glittering stones. The stockings were thigh-high and black. The three inches of lace hit just at the top of each thigh and inches from the tiny thong she had on. The scrap of lace barely covering the curls he could see were soaking wet. Her bra was also black, the lacey front only cupping the breast and leaving her nipples free. They were tight and thick and he wanted to suckle them into his mouth and make her come.

Leaning forward, he pulled her toward him, burying his face in her pussy. She rocked into his mouth, her heat, her juices soaking his chin. Moving the bit of lace from his goal with his finger he could see her hard clit peeking from her soft folds and lapped it with his tongue before pulling it into his mouth and sucking.

She came with a scream. Cream filled his mouth and he wanted more. He could feel his cock surge up. He was hard and aching again, needed to be buried deep within her. Tearing her panties from her, he pulled her down onto him and onto his cock. She tightened around him again, her head thrown back as she shouted out his name.

Pulling her hips forward, he took her nipple into his mouth and bit her. She laced her fingers into his hair and held him to her breast as she began riding him. Shamus knew that he was going to come again. He felt his cock filling with cum as he rolled her to her back and settled between her legs. As he took her mouth, devouring her, she wrapped her legs around his hips and he slammed deep as he spilled his seed into her womb. When she came again, then again, Shamus continued to pound her long after he was sated. She dropped her arms from his neck as he fell upon her, his head in the crook of her neck.

He knew he was heavy, but he couldn't move. His breathing was hitched and he wasn't sure if his heart would ever slow. But he did lift his head and look down at her. She'd either fallen asleep or had fainted. Either way, he felt a surge of incredible happiness run through him and he knew he was grinning like a fool. He just hoped he hadn't hurt her.

When she opened her eyes and looked up at him, he noticed the burns on her throat again, the bite mark on her neck that he didn't remember giving her, and her lips were swollen either from his kisses or him fucking her lovely mouth. She smiled at him and he knew he hadn't hurt her at all.

"Hi. I'm guessing you enjoyed that. I certainly did." She grinned again. "A lot."

Instead of answering her, he leaned down and gently pressed his lips to hers. When she opened under him, her tongue sliding along his, he moaned. Not from need this time, but because she'd worn him out completely.

Lifting his head, he looked down at her again. "That was incredible. The most amazing sex I've...I will ever have. You blew me away." He kissed her again and moved to the side, bringing her flush with him instead of under him. "We could probably get dressed, but I'm not sure I will ever have the energy again."

She giggled and he snuggled down next to her. Shamus watched as her eyes drifted closed, then she yawned. As he watched her she drifted off to sleep, her body so lax against his that he felt himself begin to drift. His last thought as he fell into sleep was that he was never going to be the same again.

~~~

Lilliane woke alone on the couch. The soft blanket over her made her feel warm and she smiled. There were some wonderful smells coming from what she assumed was the kitchen and she realized that she was starving. She didn't move, but lay there thinking about what she'd done.

She'd given. Not only had she given what she wanted to Shamus, but she'd done so without thought to her own pleasure. She knew what she'd done to him, knew that he was so close to taking her that she found herself wanting to bring him closer and closer until, like he'd made her do many times, he'd begged her for release. And he had. She'd loved it, she loved him.

Her breath caught as that thought came to life. She did love him. Loved him with all her being and then some, but he didn't…couldn't love her. He'd told her several times that it was going to be just temporary. That what the two of them had, what they'd been doing, was nothing more than two people coming together. She had no one to blame but herself as to what she'd done. Falling in love with Shamus McKee was going to kill her.

She felt the tears fall against her cheeks as she heard him coming toward her. Brushing them away with the blanket and pulling it up under her chin, hoping that he'd not notice she'd been crying, she smiled up at him as he leaned over the back of the couch and looked down at her.

"Hello, sleepy head. Did you have a nice nap? I did." He laid her clothes on the back of the couch. "As much as I'd like for you to remain naked I need to show you some things on the computer and, if you aren't dressed, I won't be able to concentrate. Dinner is in ten minutes."

He leaned all the way over and kissed her. It was brief, but oh so delicious. And when he started to pull away, he leaned back in for a second kiss.

"Hurry. I'm starved." He moved out of her sight just as she sat up. Watching him walk away was heating her up again and before she could do something really stupid like call him back and tell him what she'd just figured out, she grabbed her clothes and went to the little bathroom off the living area.

The woman in the mirror didn't look anything like the woman Lilliane had been used to seeing there. This woman with her tousled hair and bruised lips looked more like Sin than she had in awhile. Her sister, her twin, had that same look in her eyes now. Sated and happy, lusty and in love. As much as Lilliane liked that look, she didn't want anyone to guess at what it was. She pulled on her clothes quickly, her back turned from the mirror with purpose. When she walked into the kitchen she couldn't believe what he'd done.

There were windows all along the counter that opened to the back yard. The window sills were wide and when Cain had lived here for a while they'd been filled with an odd assortment of things. From old glass in varying hues to mugs he'd apparently collected from patients from his practice that said things like "My Favorite Doctor" to "Merry Christmas." A few even had pictures of the children, babies that he'd delivered.

Now there were small pots of plants; herbs, she assumed. Some of them with tiny flowers and others with straight stems that reached for the sun. She knew what most of them were; cilantro and dill graced one window and there was marjoram, oregano, and parsley in another. He had rosemary, sage, and basil in yet another and in the last, he had chervil, chives, and mint. And tucked in the corner next to a large food processor he had a tall bush of bay leaves. He was snipping some of the chives when he noticed her.

"I hope you're hungry. I made grilled chicken with herbs and fresh mango salad. I also grilled some potatoes, and pie for desert." He flushed. "My dad and I learned to cook or starve. He could make a mean pan of lasagna that would make your mouth water just from the ingredients."

She walked closer to the tomatoes he was cutting up and stole one. "I am hungry and this looks great. I can't remember anyone ever cooking in this kitchen when Cain lived here. He'd either order out or the girls would. We aren't a family of cooks."

"I love to play in the kitchen." He nodded to the laptop on the counter. "I need you to look at those pictures and tell me if you've ever seen any of those people before."

She walked over and sat down. Opening the computer, she saw pictures of men with numbers under their chests. She looked over at Shamus with a raised brow. "Are you trying to set me up with criminals or does this have anything to do with what happened in Tennessee? I told you, I didn't see those men."

He threw the tomatoes in a bowl with what looked like dressing and was wiping his hands as he came toward her.

"They might. Have something to do with Tennessee, I mean. These men may or may not be connected to them or the person who financed them. I just want you to look at them. And you aren't going to be dating anyone."

Her heart took a fast beat, but she cautioned it. He was talking about now, while he was still here, she was sure. He leaned over her, pointed at the first man, and said something. She couldn't hear him over the pounding of her heart. He smelled so good.

"Behave or we'll never get dinner. Look at the pictures and tell me if anyone looks familiar to you." He stepped away when she reached for him. "I mean it. I'm hungry and so are you. Look."

She sighed heavily and looked at the monitor. She didn't want to look at other men, she wanted to look at him, and preferably naked. He told her to go to the next page when she said she didn't know them.

She was on page ten when she recognized someone. "This man. I think…he might have been friends with my father. I think his name was Pollack or something."

He came toward her and clicked on the picture she indicated. "His name is Pochak. He also went by the name Crackers. We never did find out why. He was your father's cell mate. This man"—he pointed to the next picture—"was as well. They're both dead."

She looked at some more pictures and was able to pick out two more men, both also dead. They too were cell mates of her father's and she was beginning to see a pattern.

"So these men, did they supply the guns to the school shooting or was there more that I don't know?" He was dishing up the chicken off the hot grill on the stove and turned to her to hand her the plates.

"No, at least we don't think so. The first men were in on the kidnapping of your sister Quinn. The police, and rightly so, assumed that he had hired them to help him collect money he felt he was owed."

"Yes. Father thought that Alyssa owed him ten million dollars as a reward when she'd been missing. She was an heiress and, if found alive, there was a bonus. Cain got that money." She took her first bite of food and moaned. "This is delicious."

"Thanks. It's been a long time since I've had to cook for anyone, but I'm glad you like it." They ate for a few minutes before he continued. "The second three men are the ones that the army tied to the shooting of your sister Sin. That isn't public knowledge just yet so don't say anything. That equipment your brother and sister-in-law brought in came with all sorts of software that I'm sure isn't legal."

She didn't doubt that, if she wanted, Alyssa could get whatever she desired. The woman was not just rich, but scary rich. She owned more houses and property than Lilliane thought the government did.

"But my father is dead. I don't…how could he have hired people to try and kill Sin and me? Or, for that matter, where did the money come from?"

"I don't know. The only thing I can figure is that he had a partner. One that no one is aware of." He leaned back in his chair, his plate as empty as hers. "I have to be honest with you and say I thought of your mother, but…well, I'm not sure she's got the brains to do it. I'm sorry, but—"

"No, you're right. I don't think she could either. My father…Mother seemed to be devoted to him even when he beat her and, for that matter, us. I don't think my mother had a single thought that was her own the entire time I lived around here."

Shamus didn't say anything, but she could see that he agreed with her. She stood to start clearing the table. When he began helping her she told him to go sit down. He cooked, she could very well clean up. She was pleased when he sat at the counter and didn't leave.

"There has to be someone else. Someone that has a vendetta against your family. Someone with the funds to supply what is needed to get the job done and to pay some upfront money." He grinned. "I know this sounds really cold and horrible, but the person doing this is saving a great deal of money. You Waite women are really hard to get down."

She laughed. "You have no idea. There were times when my father would take the belt or his fists to us that I thought he'd kill us. But we kept bouncing back. Cain got it the worst most of the time. Father really hated him for some reason. And more so when he got the scholarship to go away to college. I think Dr. Damon had a lot to do with that."

After they finished up in the kitchen she told him she had papers to grade and he asked her if she wouldn't mind doing them in the office with him. He had some work to do as well and wouldn't mind the company. They worked in companionable silence for over two hours before they went up to bed.

He didn't ask her to stay and she didn't ask to go back to Cain's house. She wanted to spend as much time with him as she could before he finished this case. She was both dreading it and happy to see the end to come. She wanted her life back. But what sort of life would it be when he left was nothing she wanted to think about.

Chapter 15

Shamus was taking her to school the next morning when Drew called her. When she'd met with Alyssa the day before she'd asked him to take a look at the contract for her. She'd asked him to let her know as soon as possible but not to tell anyone else, please. She still wasn't sure if she was going to take the job.

Alyssa had been surprised to realize that her father had funded the school, but very happy too. She said she was going to use that as a bargaining chip if for some reason Connor didn't make it in.

"This is a very good deal. In fact, I'd like to shake hands with the person who wrote it," Drew told her. "It not only gives you one hell of a package deal, but so long as you stay and leave on good terms, your great-great-great grandchildren are able to attend free of charge. If you don't sign it, I will. Do you know how much it's going to cost to put triplets through there a year?"

Lilliane laughed. "So I should sign it? I wasn't sure about the five years. I've never worked anywhere where I had to stay a specific time length."

"They give you a good out. So long as your reasons are medical or you move you can break the contract. Also, if you decide to leave, both parties can come to an agreement there as well." He paused. "So does this mean you're staying? I haven't said anything to anyone, but I'm about to bust to tell Quinn. Or does this have anything to do with a certain cop and you?"

Lilliane glanced at Shamus. "Yes. I've got no real reason not to take it. The sale on my house is complete and..." She paused too. "And the other thing? It's just temporary."

When she closed the cell phone she was surprised when it rang again almost immediately. As she didn't answer numbers she didn't know, she most certainly didn't answer ones that were labeled "unknown" either. She directed it right to voicemail.

"You got a job offer from the school?" She looked at Shamus; his voice was sharp his tone pissed.

"Yes, they...I didn't tell you last night because you grabbed me away from my brother's house like I was a common criminal or something. Then you nearly jumped me on the stairs. After that, I got...I got distracted." She flushed when she thought of how and why she'd been distracted. "And besides, I don't believe what I have plans for after you leave has any bearing on you whatsoever."

She was glad they were pulling into the grounds to the school. As soon as he stopped she tore off her seatbelt and practically leapt from his vehicle. She didn't even slow down when he shouted her name but barged her way into the building.

She was seated at her desk ten minutes later, having stopped in the office to see if Marion was in. When she was told she wouldn't be in until eight Lilliane went to her office. But she couldn't sit still. When her phone vibrated she didn't look but took it out of her pocket and put it in the desk drawer. Before closing it she stuck her tongue out at the thing and slammed the drawer. She decided she needed a cup of tea.

The teachers' lounge was lovely. There were several vending machines that were filled daily, she'd been told. They were filled with everything from candy bars to sandwiches, though why anyone would eat from them was beyond her. They had a full serve cafeteria that was free to the staff and served a good hot meal. There were two other teachers in there and Garner.

She had just poured her hot water and sat down with that and her tea bag at an empty table when he sat down across from her. She wasn't really in the mood to deal with another male at the moment so she ignored him. Or at least she tried to.

His lewd comments were bad enough, but when he touched her thigh she'd had enough.

"Get your hand off me or, so help me, I'll hurt you." She didn't lower her voice and noticed out of the corner of her eye that the other two teachers had turned toward them.

"Ahhhh, feisty. I love it when a woman is playing hard to get. Makes the catching so much more delicious at the end, don't you think?" He squeezed her thigh, but didn't move his hand away. "What do you say we go to my office?"

"I'm not playing hard to get, you idiot. I'm telling you not to touch me. I don't want a thing to do with you. Not now, not ever." She felt her control nearly over. "Get your fucking hand off my leg."

If he hadn't laughed she might have been able to hold on, but he did. And when he moved his hand up between her legs to press against her pussy she lost it.

~~~

Alyssa called him as he was pacing the kitchen. He was mad…furious really, and didn't want to speak to anyone. And Shamus just knew that Alyssa was calling because Lilliane had called her to complain.

"I'm so sorry. I should have checked my temper at the door. She was right. About everything. Please don't fire me just yet. I need to see this thing through to the end whether she likes it or not."

The silence at the other end was profound. But before he could continue on with trying to save his ass and his job, Alyssa laughed. "Pissed you off, did she? Well that might explain some of what happened at the school." She laughed again. "Turn your phone on, Shamus. Lilliane has been trying to call you all morning."

He'd forgotten to turn it on again. When they'd gone to bed, he'd turned it to silent but not off. His heart was beating hard when he remembered she said something about the school.

"What's happened?" he asked as he grabbed his keys and headed toward his car. "Is she all right? I'm going to…where am I going?"

He was sitting in his vehicle listening to Alyssa laugh more, wondering if she'd ever calm down. He was just backing out of the garage and going to the street when she finally seemed to have control again.

"Thanks, I sincerely needed that." She let go with another laugh and a hick-uppy breath before telling him anything. "Lilliane is just fine. Better than fine, I would guess. But the guy that touched her…well, not so much. He was taken away in an ambulance and cuffs, Cait told me."

Shamus stopped at the next street and put his vehicle into park. There were no other cars around so he'd simply pulled into a parking place on the street. He was afraid of what Alyssa would tell him and he didn't want to have an accident when she did.

"This guy named Garner made a pass at her. She said he'd done it yesterday too. I take it from your growls she didn't tell you." Alyssa was laughing again and he hadn't realized he'd been growling.

"No. I'm beginning to see she doesn't tell me a great many things." He hadn't meant to sound pissy. It had already gotten him into trouble with one Waite woman and he was reasonably sure he'd just pissed off another one. Especially if the silence on the other end was any indication. "Before you blast me like I so richly deserve, I'm mad at me, not her. I don't seem to be doing so well with her."

"Do you want to?" Alyssa's question startled him, but he didn't answer before she continued. "The reason I'm asked is because I think she might be half in love with you, if not all the way."

Love? No, that couldn't be right. Women like Lilliane didn't fall for his type. "I think you're mistaken. I'm not her... She doesn't... Damn it. Lilliane deserves better than a poor beat cop that doesn't have two nickels to rub together."

She didn't say anything for a full minute. "I see. Well, she's fine at work. She just wanted me to let you know what happened before you heard about it from Cait or the news."

"Alyssa," he said quietly, knowing that she was about to hang up. "I'm not sure why you think she's in love with me. I never did anything... She knows that I'm going back. I have a job there waiting for me."

Her laughter this time was brittle and harsh. "I'm sure she's trying to tell her heart that same thing. But the funny thing about that, the heart doesn't usually give two shits what you tell it or what's in your wallet."

The phone went dead. Shamus laid his head on the steering wheel and closed his eyes. He wasn't sure what to do now. Go to the school and try and talk to her? If he did and she refused to talk to him, the school could very well ban him.

Then there was the added issue of her being hurt. He wasn't sure what he'd do if she even had a single nail broken. Alyssa said she was fine, but what did that mean? Fine because she didn't have any bullets in her or fine because she was?

He was also worried about this love thing. Lilliane couldn't be in love with him—half or otherwise. She was just infatuated with him, that's all. He'd taken her virginity and she was...she was what?

He cared for her. A great deal. She was on his mind a lot too. But she was always there because he wanted...no, he needed... No, damn it, he was being paid to protect her.

Sitting up, he opened his eyes. "Christ, I'm in love with her."

The knock at his window startled him. So much so that he reached for his weapon. The man at the window smiled and rolled his finger, indicating that he wanted Shamus to roll his down. The window was nearly down when he realized two things immediately. There were no other cars around him and the man standing there had a gun.

"You sure made this a whole lot easier than she said you might." He opened the door as Shamus pressed one on his phone. "Said you'd be a real tough one to wrangle."

Shamus heard the person answer and the second he did, Shamus spoke up. "I'm Shamus McKee. You know I'm a detective with the—"

"Yeah, yeah. Whatever, big boy. Get your ass outta the car and come on. We gots plans for you." The man reached in and grabbed Shamus' arm.

He wanted to fight back, but the gun suddenly appeared under his chin. "You wanna die here, boy, or later? Makes no never mind to us. You're a dead man anyway, hear her talk."

"She?" he asked with a hard swallow. "She who? Who wants me dead?"

"Some broad that's paying me and my friend here to bring you to her." His grin was sardonic, scary, and slightly insane. "Dead or alive."

Shamus glanced at his phone. It had gone black with disuse. He hoped that someone knew what was going on and they contacted the correct people. He hoped too that he'd be able to thank them all for their help.

"Does this have anything to do with the Waite family?" The man laughed at his question and then the earth moved. Pain in his head seemed to explode in his body. His last thought before the ground reached up and smacked him was of Lilliane.

Chapter 16

Cait looked at the truck again then walked to the rear. Something about the entire scene was off...staged, she guessed. She bent her knees and looked around. That's when she saw it. She was about to reach for it when one of her men walked up behind her.

"Captain, I have the transcript you asked for. Detective McKee did tell them right off the bat he was a cop. Said that he was working too, but they cut him off before he could tell them where."

Cait stood after pulling the metal pipe out from under his vehicle with her gloved hands. She took the sheets of paper and dropped the pipe in an evidence bag the cop was holding open for her.

"Thanks. See if you can get anything off that for me. Maybe these people were stupid enough to leave us a nice gift of their prints or something. Oh and have the photographic on my desk in an hour. There is something off by...shit. The doors were shut, weren't they? Who shuts the doors to a crime scene? Women. Tell them there was a woman at the scene, maybe the one paying the bills, and see what they can get."

She read over the transcript. The call had come in shortly after ten. The dispatcher had contacted Cait immediately then put a trace on Shamus' phone. He had saved them a great deal of time by doing that and by leaving his phone on. She just hoped it was enough. Her cell went off five minutes later.

"Please tell me what you know," Pete Shall asked. She'd notified him the minute they realized that Shamus was missing.

"There was a nine-one-one call to our office at ten-zero-three this morning. Shamus didn't answer, but did make it clear he was in distress. He did say his name to whoever it was and made sure that we could find his car. He wasn't here when we arrived. The dispatcher notified me as soon as he realized what was going down."

Peter sighed. "Damn it all to hell. Do we know yet if it was random or part of what he's working on up there?"

Cait walked away for the crime scene van pulling up before she answered. "He asked the male who took him that same thing. He wasn't answered. There were two or more men involved and I'm thinking a woman. The doors were shut when we got here."

"Yeah," Peter said with a laugh, "only a woman wants to be neat and tidy at a crime scene. Had a perp all but scrub the floor where she did in her lovers. Nasty sight. Hard to catch her when she used acid to clean up after herself. Only reason we caught her was because she ran out of acid and used bleach. Bleach doesn't get rid of the blood, only covers it up some. My plane is leaving in an hour. I should be there in two. I'm bringing what we have down here on my end—maybe we can see if we can connect some dots."

Cait didn't know what he could bring that Shamus didn't already have, but she'd welcome anything right about now. There was something wrong about this whole thing. Too many people were involved that were now dead, and who the hell was the head person?

"We're only assuming the two cases are connected. We don't have anything solid to make the rest of them work together. All we have it a bunch of seemingly random acts against a family. Not even that if you think about the attacks on Alyssa and now Shamus." Cait took a deep breath when she heard her name called and looked to see the two people she didn't need here walking toward her. "Peter, let me know when you land. I'll have someone pick you up."

Cait walked toward Cain and Alyssa. Cait had called Alyssa when she'd looked at the cell phone Shamus had left behind and saw that only a few minutes had passed between the two calls. She wanted to know what they'd said to each other.

"You didn't need to come down here. In fact, I wish that—"

"Shamus and Lilliane are seeing each other. She has to be told and she's going to want answers when we do," Cain told her. "Hell, Cait, I want them too."

A car came to a hard stop next to them and Payton and Sin got out. Cait looked at Cain. "Should I expect the rest of your family to show up as well? Damn it, this is a crime scene, not a fucking family reunion," Cait snarled before turning to the two newest arrivals. "And you two should know better."

Payton worked for her part-time. Not because she couldn't use him more, but he simply didn't want to work all the time. Being a new father and having money to burn made him a very good cop. Untouchable too. Sin worked for a large private investing firm that mostly did insurance fraud. Or so she told everyone. Cait had a feeling that the young woman did a hell of a lot more than follow men and women around to see if the insurance claim they were making was legit. Cait had a feeling that Sin Cooperider was still working for the government but didn't want her family to know.

But that didn't mean that either of them should be there.

"Ah Cap," Payton said in his best southern drawl. "You know you need us. Because Shamus is one of our own and practically family, we can't just sit around and wait for news. You know you wouldn't either."

He had a point, damn him. She herself was supposed to be off tonight and she knew that her men could do the same job she was right now. But she liked the brash young cop almost as much as she did the one standing in front of her.

And Cait knew all about the policeman's code. She herself came from a long line of cops. Her father had been one as had her uncle, and both them had been killed in the line of duty.

"All right, jackass. Sin, you should go with Cain to the school. Lilliane has had a rough morning already and this won't help. Alyssa, I need you to tell me everything you can about what you and Shamus were talking about prior to this. Payton…Payton, go and see if you can charm the crime people into giving you anything they won't give me until I have to threaten them."

Payton moved toward the van after a quick kiss to his wife. If Cait knew him like she thought she did, he'd have information for her in less than an hour. She looked at Alyssa and Cain.

"This is all I have right now…"

~~~

Ten more minutes. Ten more minutes and she'd be able to go home. Not the home she wanted to go to, but at her brother's house. She glanced at the clock again.

The thing with Garner this morning upset her more than she thought possible. She didn't want to be known as a violent person, but he'd just pushed her buttons.

When he'd touched her so indecently, especially when she'd told him several times to stop, she'd been more embarrassed than anything. But then she'd gotten mad. She was really glad that Sin had taught her how to fight and to fight dirty.

She'd come around in a round-house punch that caught him square in the nose. After the blood erupted and spilled on his chin he'd come at her with his fists. She picked up her mug by the handle and used it like an extension to her arm and slammed the pottery into his face. Dropping the broken pieces, she brought her foot up, connected with his nuts, and lifted him off the floor. He dropped, screaming. It took Lilliane a few seconds to realize that she'd been pulled away by the two teachers there with them and held back.

Marion came in just after the police arrived.

Lilliane didn't lose her job. Nor was the school pressing charges against her. So long as she pressed charges against Garner. She'd been a bit stunned by that, but had done as they asked. She would have anyway. No one should be allowed to get away with something so horrible.

It was small wonder that Shamus didn't take her calls. She was a royal bitch and had been very nasty to him. She should have told him. She felt her phone vibrate in her pants pocket and pulled it out.

There was a voicemail and a text message. She had forgotten about the call this morning. She laid the phone on her desk and pulled up the text. While it was loading up the bell rang. Freedom!

It took her twenty minutes to empty her room of students and then another ten to get it set back to rights. It was Friday and she had the whole weekend ahead of her to make things right with Shamus. She was just reaching for her phone again when her brother and sister walked in.

Lilliane knew immediately that something had happened. She sat down hard on her desk chair. Sin came forward and took both her hands into hers.

"We know very little, but you have to stay with me. We don't know anything much, but we can't assume the worst, right?"

Lilliane nodded. "Who?" She knew. It was Shamus and something had happened to him because of her. Sin confirmed it.

"He called the police as it was going down. Shamus was smart, he didn't resist so we assume he was alive when they took him. Lilly Pad, did anything happen on the way here this morning?"

"We had…I was mad at him. He was upset and I… Oh Sin, did they take him because of me? They did, didn't they?"

Cain came forward then. "We don't know, honey. Cait is working on it right now. I'm going to take you back to your house and—"

"No. I want to go to… I need to be near where he was. He might…they might call and he lived there. Please, Cain, take me back to the house."

Cain nodded and she stood. Her cell phone ringing startled her. When she looked down and saw "unknown," she started to answer it, but it suddenly cut off.

"I had a text earlier. Maybe it was from whoever took him." She opened the tab to turn on the phone just as the voicemail alert sounded. "Oh my God."

The phone tumbled out of her hand and she dropped back into the chair. Sin grabbed the phone before it hit the floor. Lilliane felt the room spin and before she could slip away into the darkness reaching up to her, someone was pressing her head between her knees.

"Take deep breaths, baby. Come on. Don't faint on me now," Cain was telling her. "Lilly Pad we need you to stay with us. Sin is calling Payton. Come on now. Breathe."

"They've hurt him," she sobbed to her brother. "He… They hurt him so badly."

"I know, sweetheart. You need to say with me." Cain pressed her down again when she tried to rise up. "Not yet. You may be fine, but I'm not yet, so let me hold you there a bit longer so I don't faint on you."

She giggled like she was sure he'd meant for her to do. She told him she wanted to sit up when he was ready and he let her. But he stood close to her. She noticed that her phone was missing and asked him about it.

"Sin took it. She called Payton and he asked her to tell him about…about stuff." Cain sat on the edge of her desk. "They'll find him. He's strong and healthy. We'll get him back for you."

Lilliane only nodded. She wanted to ask for her phone back, but was afraid to look at the picture of Shamus again. He'd been beaten so badly. Even the quick glimpse showed that he was bleeding and that he'd been tied up. She was worried about him being in pain, wanted to go and find him right now.

When Sin came back, she looked worried. "The phone has two messages, but without…we need to know if they contacted you. Could you… Payton doesn't want you to listen to them, Lilly Pad, but I told him to fuck off."

Lilliane grinned. "I'm sure you did. And I'm also sure that there was more to it than that. Give me my phone, please. I need to know anyway."

The first one was a hang up without leaving anything. The second one, the last call, wasn't. It was very detailed about what they were going to do to Shamus if she didn't cooperate with them. Lilliane knew whatever they wanted, she'd do.

"I got him, you fucking cunt. I got your lover boy and if you don't want me to break him more you'll start answering your fucking phone when I call you. I'll give you one more chance to save his sorry ass. I'll call you at six o'clock on this line and you'd better fucking answer or he'll be hurting."

The scream that followed made her ill. She knew it was Shamus even before the voice came back on the line.

"You'll do as I say or else. You contact the police and he's dead. Cop boy lives or dies by your decisions."

The line went dead.

Lilliane sat on the couch and listened to the noise around her. She supposed it was conversations, but to her right now it was simply noise. She looked at Jazzie when she sat down beside her and took her hand.

Neither of them spoke. There really weren't any words that needed to be said, not really. But Lilliane did appreciate the comfort. She watched as Cait made her way toward them with Peter.

He'd arrived an hour ago, about two hours since the message had been discovered. She hadn't really connected him with the man from Tennessee, the other cop from the hospital, but there were so many men and women running around it was small wonder she could pick out her family. They were making use of the equipment and the endless food that was being prepared. Cait sat down.

"How you holding up, kid?" Lilliane shrugged. "I'd probably be a basket case too."

"What have you found out?" Lilliane turned to Jazzie when she asked, grateful for her sister.

"Lots, actually." Cait hesitated. Lilliane knew whatever was next, she wasn't going to like it. "We figure they are going to want you to come to them. Probably do an exchange. We've talked it over and...well, we thought maybe we'd send Sin instead of you. She had—"

"A child. No. I'm not risking my sister's life. If they want me then—"

"Lilliane, she's more experienced. She can handle a gun. She can fight back. She stands a better chance of coming out alive than you do." Lilliane turned from Cait to look at her twin before looking back at Cait.

"She doesn't agree with you either." Lilliane watched the flush on Cait's face bloom. "I killed those other men. The ones that came to the school. Why don't you think I can do this?"

"You were lucky then, damned lucky. Lilliane, damn it, this is a police matter. You'll have to do this my way." Cait got up and started pacing. "You're a school teacher, your sister is special forces personnel. When they call you'll tell them what they want and we'll handle it from there."

146

Chapter 17

Ginny sat in the chair and watched the cop. He hadn't moved once since those idiots had brought him to her. They'd beaten him up when he'd tried to overpower them. They told her that they hadn't expected him to wake up so soon. Stupid. Stupid. Stupid.

She glanced over at the body on the other side of the room from them. He probably hadn't expected her to kill him either, she thought with a small laugh. When he'd gotten in her face about people killing cops and how much more aggressive they became when one of their own was hurt or killed, she'd snapped. Well, not really snapped. She'd been looking for a way to narrow down the number of people who knew what she'd planned and he'd just made her pissed enough to do him first.

Curtis and his dead buddy, Benny, had a lot to answer for if the big time cop didn't wake up. She needed him to tell the teacher to get her ass here and save his butt. He might need a little help with that and she was fully prepared to shoot him wherever brought the most screams from him in order to do it.

Ginny glanced at her watch. Forty-five minutes until she had to call. She wondered what Guinevere was thinking about all this and hoped she'd keep her mouth shut. Guinevere didn't much care for Ginny's plan concerning the cop.

They had fought about it bitterly. Guinevere thought they should just wait and see. Ginny had asked her for what.

"You think that money-grubbing whore is going to suddenly keel over and die? Or do you honestly think your son is going to suddenly have a change of heart and give you what you want?" Guinevere was starting to nod when Ginny laughed. "You really are stupid, aren't you?"

"I wish I'd never found... Cain loves me. I'm his mother and little boys love their mothers above all else. If it wasn't for that woman he'd—"

"He'd nothing, and you know it. He doesn't have any respect for you. Hell, I'd venture to say that he doesn't even love you anymore, if he ever did. You killed that a long time before you found me."

Ginny could almost feel the other woman's anger. Hot and immediate, it seemed to make Guinevere brave for just a second or two. When she lashed back at Ginny she laughed, her own anger just as volatile.

"You keep yourself under control or you'll be sorry. And you know exactly what I'm talking about. You know that I'll do it for good this time. I won't have you fucking up my plans."

Yes, Guinevere had known what she'd meant because as she went away, Ginny knew she was afraid. Ginny didn't like to use that threat often, but if it worked then so be it. Ginny made a mental note to use it again when she got out of line. She looked over again at the man on the floor when he moaned.

"You'll lay there or die right now," Ginny spoke through the voice modulator. It was perhaps the best ten bucks she'd ever spent in the toy department at Wally-World. She stood up and touched the barrel of the Glock to his injured cheek. She smiled when he flinched away from it. Good, she wanted him to know who was in charge.

"Lilliane?" he asked, though she wasn't sure how with his jaw broken. Apparently Curtis had been wrong about that. She'd have to have a little talk with the bastard when he returned. She was suddenly glad for the blindfold she'd had Curtis put on the cop before he'd left.

"Your cunt? No, I don't have her. Not yet anyway. But soon, mark my words. And when I do…well, I was going to tell you that I would set you free, but we both know that's not going to happen."

She didn't think he'd run back home with his tail between his legs like Guinevere had said he would. Ginny was pretty sure the man was in love with the teacher and he'd have to avenge her death or some stupid thing like that. Love was the dumbest thing in the world, she thought. Ginny knew her plan was perfect—bring the teacher here then let her watch as she murdered her lover. Then kill the teacher. But she had a small twinge of…fear?

"Why?" he asked her, bringing her out of her thoughts.

Why indeed, she mused. Again, the small brush of that feeling returned. This time, however, instead of letting it settle over her, she let it piss her off.

"Because I want all of them dead. Then I'm gonna fuck Cain before I slit his throat. Maybe even during his release. Wouldn't that be grand?" Ginny got up and kicked the cop twice in the ribs. "But you, you cock sucker, are going to be dead long before he will be."

When he reached out and snatched her leg, grabbing her ankle tight, she fell. He was on her in a heartbeat. He might have gotten the blindfold off just then but for Curtis coming in at that moment and hitting him in the head again.

"You okay?" She looked up at Curtis from the chair again. She was well away from the cop and Curtis while he tied the cop up. Ginny wanted him dead, she wanted the cop dead right fucking now. But she needed him. At least for now.

"Fine. I thought you said he was too injured to move? You also said his jaw was broken. If it is then he's a fucking miracle because he talked to me just fine with it."

Curtis looked back at the cop before answering her. "He's not going to move now and I told you I thought his jaw was broken. Benny hit him really hard."

Ginny wanted to snarl at the stupid man then kill him, but like the cop, she needed him too. She looked pointedly at his dead friend.

"You want to end up like him then keep making stupid mistakes. I told you before we need to be careful. If even one of those fucking brats of hers finds out who I am they'll be able to trace her back to me. Then on back the line to you and you'll get nothing because I'll have nothing in prison."

He nodded. Little did he know he wasn't going to get dick anyway. He'd be just as dead as the teacher, cop, and his poor dead friend long before she and Guinevere had all the money they could ever want.

After telling Curtis she needed to go out and to watch the cop, she went to the hole that Guinevere's son had so generously gotten for them—not, she thought with a snarl.

She supposed that by most standards the house wouldn't be considered all that bad. But it wasn't the house that Cain and the money-grubbing whore had. That's what she wanted. Not this…hovel.

The hovel had four bedrooms, of course, but there was no maid service to clean up after them. There were also five bathrooms, but since neither she nor Guinevere were much on house work, the bathrooms had taken a decidedly bad turn. The only one that was reasonably clean was the one in Guinevere's room and Ginny had to sneak in there to use it.

In addition to the big kitchen that no one used, there was a living room, family room, and also a big office. The latter room had become their planning room and it was covered in pictures of the kids, newspaper clippings, and also a list of ways they wanted them dead. So far, the list had been the only thing they'd been able to accomplish with not any follow through. The four-car garage was empty of anything drivable, and even if there was a really nice car there to ride in there wasn't a driver to take them anywhere anyway. All in all, the place was a dump.

Ginny wanted it all and wouldn't be satisfied until she…they had it all. Smiling, Ginny thought about Guinevere.

"Soon," she said softly so that the other woman wouldn't hear her. "Soon you will have worn out your welcome and I'll take care of you too."

~~~

Lilliane finally got Sin alone. Her sister seemed to realize that she was trying to talk to her privately and had been avoiding her. Well, now she had her—as soon as she came out of the flipping bathroom.

The door opened and Lilliane rushed her back inside. Sin didn't fight, just simply let her shut the door and lock it. Sin smiled.

"I agree with you. I don't have to like it, but they're right and you know it," Sin said as she hopped up on the counter.

That took Lilliane back. "Then you'll let me go and get him. I have to."

"No. I didn't say that. I said I agree with you. I don't want you hurt any more than you do me." Sin shook her head. "Look, Lilly, these people are playing for keeps. They had no trouble taking a good cop out of his own vehicle. What the hell do you think they'll do to you?"

Lilliane had thought of that. "And if it was Payton and you and I were to switch? You'd just let me go in without you?"

"But we aren't," Sin said softly. "Look, sis, this is the best way. I'll bring him back to you and—"

"I'll follow you." Lilliane nearly burst out laughing at the look on her sister's face. "I'm going to know where you're going. They're going to call me, remember? So you let me go with you or for you or I go on my own. You know I will too."

Sin sat there for several seconds cussing a blue streak. Lilliane knew she had her when she glared and pulled her leg up. She pulled up her pant leg and continued to glare as she unbuckled the holster around her ankle.

"I told Payton this wouldn't work. I told him you were just enough like me and if it wouldn't fly by me, it wouldn't you either." She handed her the gun and then the larger Glock at the back of her pants. "You remember how to use these?"

"Yes. Head and chest, largest areas to hit. Go for the kill and don't stop firing until I run out of ammo or the threat is dead. Don't bring a squirt gun to a gun fight."

Sin grinned. "I meant how to fire them. But that'll do too." Sin stood up and started taking off her shirt while going over all the things she'd taught her years ago about surviving and how to fight. Lilliane had been a good pupil, she never missed a one. In ten minutes they not only changed clothes, but identities.

They'd done this before, switched who they were or simply became the other. Lilliane had done it for Sin more than the other way around. Sin would make two dates and she'd take one and Lilliane the other. It was fun and if not for Sin's "double dates," Shy Lilly, as she'd been called, wouldn't have dated all that much, if at all. Lilliane had often wondered if she'd done it to make sure Lilliane went out once in awhile.

But the time they'd gone back to the living room Lilliane had slipped into being her sister. She knew that not even Cain could tell them apart because he had never been able to before. Payton, she realized the moment she sat down next to him, knew immediately.

Lilliane waited for him to say something. Anything that would rat them out, but he didn't. He handed her Tonya and kissed Lilliane hard on the mouth.

"She told me you wouldn't let her go," he whispered. "But you get hurt and I will personally kick your ass, and hers too."

For the next eight minutes—the longest in her life—Lilliane tried to calm herself by playing with her niece Tonya. When her phone rang, she nearly reached for it, but Payton put his hand on her leg then took her hand. Sin answered.

They'd given her, now Sin, a list of things to say and to ask. The plan was to try and keep them on the phone as long as possible. Cait said it would more than likely be another pay as you go phone, but maybe not. Lilliane listened to this end of Sin's conversation.

"I want to talk to Shamus." Then, "How do I know you even have Shamus then? I want to talk to Shamus, please." Lilliane wanted to snatch the phone away when Sin nodded. "Are you all right?"

Lilliane got up, went to her sister's side, and leaned against her trying to hear. But she could only hear the voice again, the one that had left the voice message.

"Listen, teach, you'll do just what I tell you to do or he's dead. You come to the mall in one hour and wait for someone to come and get you. Once they tell you where he is, you'll come to me. Now here is what I want. Do you got a pencil?"

"Yes. Tell me what you want. Just don't…please don't hurt Shamus again." Sin had been told to say his name a lot, but not her own. "Shamus means the world to me. I love Shamus very much." Sin sat down to write whatever the person said as if there weren't twenty other people listening in on the conversation with her.

"One hundred million dollars. And there had better not be one—"

"I don't have that sort of money. Even if I did, I couldn't get it in o—"

"You'll get it, bitch, or you might as well bring a gun and put a bullet in the cop's head. Do I make myself clear?"

The bite in Sin's voice was sharp. "Yes. Crystal."

"Let me see… Oh. One hundred million dollars. And there had better not be one of those bottles to spray on us…me when I open it either. It needs to be in a sack…no, satchel with no locks. One hour." Then the line went dead.

No one said a word for several seconds; the silence was deafening. Then as quiet as the room had been, the noise that broke open was just as profound. Payton pulled her back to the couch with him and Sin sat next to her.

Cait and Peter stood before them. When Payton took her hand again, she started to pull away, but he simply tightened his grip on her fingers. She was glad for it seconds later when Cait started talking to her as Sin. And had he not pinched her fingers, she wouldn't have answered correctly.

"Yes, I have my weapons. But don't you think they'll expect me to be armed?" She would, Sin was always armed.

"Maybe you," Cait laughed. "But not a kindergarten teacher. Lilliane doesn't carry a gun, nor does she fight back. That's what they'll expect. That's why this is such a great idea."

"I still think I should go. What if they ask me something personal about Shamus and she doesn't know the answer?"

Lilliane started to snap at her sister when again Payton pinched her fingers. She decided that when this was over, she was going to buy him something really nice and expensive for all his help. Then she was going to beat him over the head with it. Her fingers were hurting already.

Alyssa sat down on the coffee table when Cait left after one of the other police called for her and Peter. She handed her Connor. He started playing with the button on her shirt when Alyssa started laughing. Lilliane looked at her confused.

"You can fool the adults but not the children," Alyssa said softly then took Connor back as she stood. "Just so you know, I would have done the same thing. Don't get hurt, sweetheart, and bring Shamus back to us."

Lilliane nodded. "I will. But I don't…the money. What are we going about—"

"You let them worry about that." Alyssa nodded to the other room and headed that way, Cain right behind her. "They figured on wanting money. They've been preparing it since you got here."

Lilliane burst out laughing when she saw how they'd "prepared" the money. Quinn's triplets and then Connor were playing with it in the big play pen in the den. They were making the fake one thousand and five hundred dollar bills distressed by rolling on it, eating it, and basically being babies with it.

"This is the final batch. We had to print several hundred sheets of them to get what we might need. Then cut them out," Cain told her. "There are nine cops in the other room putting them in neat stacks."

"How many laws are you breaking by doing this? At least two that I can think of." She looked at the one he took out of Connor's mouth and handed it her.

"None. See." It took her several seconds to see. "It's Alyssa's dad one Halloween before he died. He's dressed up as Grover Cleveland."

Instead of facing the right, Nathan Howard was facing forward. The huge grin on his face should have clued her in, but she'd missed that too. When Cain flipped it over, she laughed. That too had been changed. The words "The United States of America" had been replaced with "The United Kingdom of Atlantis."

Lilliane had never actually seen a thousand dollar bill before, only in pictures, but she thought it looked all right. Even the colors looked to be about what she'd think they should be. There were several bags and suitcases in the room with the officers too. She looked over at her brother.

"Nathan was always prepared for this to happen. He was a very wealthy man and knew that someday he'd have to pay a ransom or his family would. In the event of it happening, he was always coming up with plans to make it run smoothly. Alyssa said before he died he used to tell her just how to handle it in the event he was taken." Cain brushed his fingers down her cheek before he continued. "You're great for doing this, Sin. I don't want anything to happen to either of you, but you're the one who will take care of this if it can be done."

She looked into his eyes. He was telling her…Sin to kill them. Lillian swallowed hard. Could she?

She'd done it before, not with purpose, really, but she had. She looked in the other room where the babies played. Tonya, Sin's daughter, had joined the children. If this person finally did get one of them, one of the adult's, one or more of those children would grow up without a parent. She couldn't let that happen if she could help it. She looked back at her brother.

"I understand. And you're right. I can and will take care of this if I can."

Chapter 18

Shamus woke slowly, but didn't move. He didn't want to piss off the person who had him any more than he already had. Christ, he hurt.

His head hurt like someone had pounded on it. Not once, but twice. Oh yeah, he thought sardonically, they had. He was glad for the blindfold that covered his eyes for he was sure that any light coming in would have felt like a dagger in his skull.

He was reasonably sure he had some broken ribs. Every breath he took felt as if a chain saw was cutting through him. Even shallow breaths hurt like a mother fucker. He wiggled his toes carefully inside of his boots.

There was pain there. Not like his ribs, but enough that he knew walking was going to be slow and painful. From the pressure around his ankles he surmised he'd been tied up. His wrists too. Moving his fingers one at a time caused sweat to pop on his brow that he could feel beading down his face. Two, maybe three fingers were broken, two more close. His arms, like his legs, were hurt but not enough to incapacitate him.

Shamus knew if he had to fight he could, but he also knew he may die anyway. He needed to get to Lilliane, knew if nothing else he had to tell her that he loved her. A noise alerted him he was about to have company.

The person didn't speak so he assumed he was alone. Shamus hoped he'd hear voices so he could figure out who had him, but all he got was some shuffling around and some heavy breathing. Then Shamus heard something being dragged across the room.

Shamus wasn't sure why he thought it was a body, but he did. So when a male spoke, he wasn't surprised by what he was saying.

"Benny, Benny, Benny. You shouldn't of autta pissed her off. I told you fifty times to a hundred that one has a short temper and a quicker fuse. I said to be quiet around that one and now look at you." Something heavy dropped. "You've gone and got yourself all dead."

So the woman had killed Benny. Good to know. If she was willing to pull the trigger on someone she knew, she'd have no problem pulling it on a stranger. Shamus thought of a few other things as well, but didn't have time to think all of them through right now.

The one or two things he knew were that first this man and the now dead Benny had known each other for some time, more than a few months anyway. And they didn't know the woman well at all. Benny would have known about her temper and would have been more cautious. But Benny and this man had discussed her without her knowledge so they didn't live together. If they had, they'd both be dead instead of just one of them because Shamus figured that they would have already pissed her off before now.

The person in charge was a woman, which in itself was different. Women didn't usually gather a click or group to do the job. They usually acted alone or had a male that they deferred to for guidance. Which lead him to believe she was older, maybe in her late forties to fifties. Probably educated, but not too much beyond a year of college if even that much.

The short fuse could mean she was pissed off at these two for botching up something. Or, and this would be his best guess, she was unstable. Not many people would kidnap a cop and expect to get away with it. So she had to be nuttier than a bowl of Planters.

A kick to his foot sent a pain up through his body like a shard of glass, all the way to his head. The moan poured from him before he could get it to stop. Shamus had to take several deep breaths before he could even consider moving again. He didn't get the chance to try and compartmentalize the pain.

"Get up, Shamus. The lady wants you to take a walk." Shamus nearly missed the man's muttering. "Why she don't just leave him here is beyond me. Save me halfin' to drag his body back down again."

The man jerked him upright and the blindfold slipped down off his eyes. Shamus got a good look at not just the man who had taken him from his vehicle, but also the dead man across from them. Shamus snapped his eyes closed when the man started to turn toward him again.

Holy Christ, the dead Benny was a cop.

~~~

Lilliane was sitting in the food court at eight-thirty. In another thirty minutes someone was supposed to sit with her and then he'd take the money. Then she was supposed to see Shamus.

She looked at the paper cup in front of her and took another deep breath. She knew that the chances of her actually seeing Shamus were nil to none. A small giggle escaped her before she could stop it. Zero to none was about right.

She looked down at the backpack at her feet. It did have some real money in it. So much so it was a little staggering. Almost a hundred grand, Payton had told her.

"Just in case they check harder than with just their eye. The person who called was reading from a script, we believe, and it's a male. The one in charge of this whole thing is a female."

"Isn't that unusual? I mean, aren't men predominately the ones who commit serial murders?" She flushed when he smiled at her like he was proud. "I guess watching all those crime shows paid off."

"Yes. But it does happen." He handed her the transcripts from her phone call and another from Cain's. "All the calls are from the same phone. We've been able to pinpoint a location as local, but not much more than that. So you need to be careful. This person is not just nuts, Lilly, but fucking, off the chart nuts."

She laughed. "So is that a police term or have you been reading the thesaurus again?" She kissed his cheek. "I'll be careful. I promise."

And now here she was. Glancing at her watch she noticed that it was now twenty-five minutes to go. She looked up and saw a man staring at her very intently.

Lilliane tried to think like Sin or even one of the other two cops she now knew. She decided that Sin would have gotten up and gone over to confront the man, then she would have kicked his ass if he didn't give her the right answer. Then she realized for the moment, she was Sin. She started to rise when someone sat in front of her.

He laid a gun and a small computer on the table. Lilliane looked up at his face, or what she could see of it. He had on a knitted hat that had only the eyes cut out. They were looking back at her with so much hostility that she nearly flinched from them. The dark color looked so stark against the paleness of the part of his face that she could see. She reached down and turned the cup in front of her just a little more.

"Got the money?" His voice sounded normal, not like it did on the phone. She nodded. "Good. Slide it over here and—"

"Where's Shamus? You said I'd get to see Shamus." She hooked her foot around the backpack and drew it toward her. "No Shamus, then you get no money."

He cursed then jerked the small computer he'd put on the table toward him. He turned it facing her after he played around with it for several seconds. The picture there had her suck in a deep breath. Shamus. The blindfold was covering most of his face, but not too much where she couldn't see who he was. She could also see the blood on his leg and the tightness in his face. He looked to her like he was in a great deal of pain.

"He can hear you. And if you try anything stupid, I'll walk away and you'll not know where he is. Got it, sister?"

She nodded. Her mind was working frantically to try and figure out what to ask him without Mr. Cap knowing what she was doing. She knew she probably only had one or two minutes at best.

"Shamus, are you all right?"

"Lilliane? Where are you? You have to get out of here. This is no place for a woman like you."

"Not there. I guess you know what's going down. I'm giving them what they want to get you out of there." His body stiffened, but he didn't say anything and she continued. "Alyssa gave me the money. I've never seen so many Grants in my entire life."

He nodded before answering. "I bet. Those Grants...who was the traitor again? Was it Benjamin Franklin?"

She frowned. "No. His name was Arnold, Benedict Arnold. I'm going to bring you home. Then you'll be fine."

"Don't. Lying doesn't become you." He shifted on his seat. "When this is over, we're just where we said we'd be, over. You go back to where you want and I'll finally get my promotion. All I ever wanted, kiddo."

The pain to her heart was like a physical lash. She nodded to the camera before she remembered he couldn't see her. "I see.

Well, you did make that perfectly clear, didn't you? I'm going to give him the money and when he's satisfied then you'll be free."

Blindly, she kicked the money to the man in front of her while looking at the man on the screen. She wasn't sure what to do now and thought maybe it didn't really matter. She nearly picked up the paper cup in front of her before she remembered that it had to stay put. When the man stood, so did she. He closed the computer and picked up the gun.

"Come on, girly. You and me got places to go." He motioned her to precede him with a wave of the gun and she did, reaching for the cup again.

The walk to the doors was short. She'd sat just where she'd been told and was soon out into the night air. The rain falling on her face was cold, but she hardly felt it. Her entire body felt like she'd been run over. Before she could think about what she was doing, she was being shoved into a car.

"Where are you taking me," she asked him when he opened the driver's side door and climbed in, throwing the pack in the back.

"To the cop. Though I don't think the lady is going to be happy about this. She seemed to think you and the man were lovers." She didn't say anything and he continued. "Course, she ain't had all that much right so far anyway."

"Why does she want me?" The man glanced at her question. "I mean, she took Shamus so that she could have me. I'm not that stupid."

"Don't know really. She seems to have a bug up her ass about all you guys. Don't know what you'ins did to piss her off, but it must have been big." He turned back toward the highway when they left the mall parking lot. "I'm supposed to take you to her and that cop...I suppose she'll let you know when you get there."

Lilliane nodded and took a drink of the empty cup—well, of liquid anyway. The small camera inside was recording everything they said and did. She had been both impressed and terrified when Sin told her how it worked.

"I can pick up anything from a rat farting to you traveling to the moon—at least to the next state anyway with the camera and mike in the cup." Sin pulled another box from her pocket. "And this baby will tell me where you are if you get separated from the cup. I can lose the camera, but not you."

The small pin was beautiful and nothing like she'd ever expect her sister to wear. With a wink Sin explained how she "happened" to have it.

"When I was over in the...when I was working last week, one of the...people I was working with showed me this. It was attached to someone we'd been chasing for a few days. She didn't need it anymore so I misappropriated it for me. The goons in the other room were able to pick up the feed and now you are just a click or two away from me at all times."

Lilliane put her hand on her sister's and looked her in the eye. They all had figured that Sin was doing something more than just being a consultant. She had been limping last week and had tried to brush it off as her old injuries acting up. But right at this moment, Lilliane knew.

"Are you being careful too?" she'd asked her quietly. "I can't...I won't lose you either."

"I'm very careful. I promise you. If I get hurt Coop said he'd kick my ass and that of my commanding officer." She looked around the room then back at Lilliane. "I'm working with Patterson. He keeps me safe too." Lieutenant Colonel David Patterson, her old boss in the Special Forces, would not let anything happen to his favorite person again. Once was enough for them all.

Lilliane turned it so that it could see where they were going. She took a deep breath and sighed. Shamus was well on his way to being free and so was she. She wondered if it would hurt any less once this was over.

The house wasn't what she'd expected. It was a nice two-story that sat in an open lot with nothing on either side of it. There might have been something there at one time on the right, but the left was a beautiful open area that looked like it might have had a very nice garden set in it. Lilliane looked up at the man when he told her to get the hell out.

She got out and stood. When she started to stretch, she set the cup on the roof of the car. After a couple of slow turns of it that she hoped looked like she couldn't get it to set up right, she raised her arms over her head and reached for the sky. Lilliane hoped that with the view from the camera they would be able to see what she was seeing and come for them both. She was as ready as she'd ever be, she supposed, and she lowered her hands she removed the pin from her shirt. Time to free Shamus.

Chapter 19

Shamus heard someone come up on the porch, but couldn't tell who. Not that it mattered. All he could think about was what he'd said to Lilliane. He only hoped she understood that he'd been trying to save her ass. The less they thought they were in love, the more likely they'd let her go instead of keeping her.

In his heart he knew that they were going to kill them both and there wasn't a damned thing he could do about it. The noise at the door startled him and he cocked his head that way.

He wanted to get up and see, but he was still tied to the fucking chair. Not that he thought he could walk anyway. And he knew that he was losing too much blood. He had been drifting in and out of consciousness since Lilliane had stopped talking to him.

He'd been told that the camera was on him and he'd tried his best to sit up straighter and not show his pain so much. The voice had told him that he'd be talking to Lilliane and that he'd better watch what was said. He felt the muzzle of the gun press into his thigh seconds before the pain exploded. He screamed out in pain and nearly passed out from it.

"The teach has to know I've been treating you poorly or she might not want to come so quickly and save your ass. Can't have that now, can we? I've been working too hard to get this thing rolling to have some dick like you fuck it up." The gun pressed to his temple. "If you so much as hint at what you think you might know, I'm going to blow your fucking head off while your little cunt watches in Technicolor."

"The teacher," Shamus said through a haze of pain. "We're not lovers. I was told to watch over her and her brother made it clear she was—"

"I know what I saw." Something hard slammed against his head and he felt the blood flow down his cheek. "You two can barely keep your hands off each other. You think I'm stupid."

She'd seen them together. His mind registered this seconds before something slammed into his head again. He slipped away, no more than a second or two; he knew because she was speaking to him again.

"—this is going to work. If it doesn't then you're a dead man. If it does then," her laughter rang in his head, "you're still a dead man."

The door opening had him tense as it brought him from his thoughts. He felt someone take his pulse, but they didn't speak. It wasn't until he smelled her perfume that he realized who was with him.

"I thought I told you to stay away from—"

"It's Sin. Shut up and listen. You're alone in this house?" He shrugged then moaned. "Sit tight."

He would have laughed if he didn't hurt so much. Shamus woke when someone shook him slightly. He tried to fight the darkness, but it was winning.

"Where's Lilliane? She was with someone and they—"

"Lilliane is home. You've been talking with me. As for the ass wipe I was with, he's no longer a problem. The guy in the basement? Know what happened to him?"

"The woman...he works for, I mean, he worked for Cait. He's a cop that had been helping me out with the covert of your sister. The other guy...the one you took care of, they were partners and he told me that she killed him. He said something about him pissing her off. I don't know what for, though. Is she all right?"

She ignored his question. "I'm not taking you out of here. But the men in white are on their way to get you. I'm going to go and…I'm going to find the grand dame and see if I can talk some sense into her."

He could hear the sirens coming and wondered fleetingly if they were coming now. He felt himself slipping further away. He wanted to say something to Sin, to tell her something, but he couldn't seem to focus. The sharp command telling him to "wake the fuck up" from her had him try and straighten up again.

"You die before someone can interrogate you and Cait is going to be pissed. She had a few questions to ask you and she'll kick my ass if you can't." He heard her moving around.

"Take off the blindfold. I can't see." He waited for her to comply. "Hello? Is there anyone here?"

Before he drifted off again, Shamus had a feeling she was standing right there and had ignored him. He was going to so kick her ass when he was better. He just hoped he lived long enough to follow through on it.

~~~

Lilliane sat down on the couch and listened to Shamus. She watched him as he shouted for her, but she didn't answer. She wiped at the tears as they fell across her cheeks and stained her shirt. She wanted to reach out and pull him to her, but knew that if she did not only would he know she wasn't her sister, but she didn't think she would be able to let him go. She turned to the door again when she realized she needed to get going and stepped over the inert body of the man on the porch. Killing him had made her feel badly for all of ten seconds.

He'd gotten her up on the porch by yanking her around like a rag doll. Then stuck the gun into her neck from behind. She didn't move until she felt his breath on her neck. His whispered comment made her skin crawl and her heart pound.

"We, you and I, we're going to have us some fun before the bitch gets back. If she's in there, then maybe we can have her join us. Might make for a fun afternoon if'n you know what I mean."

Her elbow came back quick and right into his breast bone. When he staggered slightly, she turned into him with her hand raised. She slammed the palm of her hand into his nose as hard as she could. She felt the bones break and move under her hand. When he dropped back and then to his knees, she was shocked at how easy that had been. Then she was appalled at herself for thinking that. She reached down and felt for a pulse and wasn't surprised to not find one. That move was the first one Sin had taught her and the hardest to get right. She'd been lucky this time.

When Shamus fell quiet for more than two minutes, she got up and checked his pulse again. It was still beating but not very strong. It took her a few minutes to bind up is leg to stop the bleeding. She was worried for a second then heard the police outside the house and knew he'd be all right.

She went to the door as her sister had told her to do and opened it wide. Only after she tossed out her gun did she shout she was alone and coming out, stepping over the inert body of the man who she'd killed. They, of course, rushed her and tossed her to the porch before she was out the door more than a foot.

Lilliane didn't fight them. She knew what to expect. She'd been drilled several times by first her sister then Payton on what to do and not to do. She knew that her best bet was to let them do their job and she'd live a lot longer. It wasn't until Cait Grant came onto the porch that Lilliane was let up.

"You all right, Lilliane? The medics can have a look at you after they finish up with McKee." She shook her head. "All the same, I'm supposed to make sure you go to the hospital after I'm finished with you. My brother-in-law Damon is going to have a look at you when you get there."

Lilliane nodded again. "That man there." She pointed to the body. "I killed him. I probably could have just hurt him, but...I had to get inside and he was going to be a problem still breathing." She looked up sharply when she realized what she'd called her.

"Yeah, I knew. Your sister told me about an hour ago. What the fuck were you two thinking anyway? You could have fucking been killed." Cait crouched down to her level on the floor. "Your brother knows too and he is so not a happy camper."

Lilliane laughed. She couldn't help it. "You know, I'm sick to death of people thinking I'm some sort of pansy-assed girly girl. I did all right on my own, didn't I? So, Captain Grant, I'd like it very much if you and the others just back the fuck up."

Cait watched her for a second or two then threw back her head and laughed. She stood up then and put her hand out to Lilliane to help her stand. She was still laughing when she cuffed her and read her her rights. This, too, was something she expected. One just did not murder people without there being consequences.

She was sitting in the jail cell three hours later when Drew showed up. He looked as pissed as she felt. When the officer opened the cell door she slipped out only to be pulled into his arms and hugged. She held on to him, suddenly needing the contact more than she'd realized. When he stepped back she knew he was still mad, but he seemed to have a better control.

"I'm to take you to the hospital. Cait said she'd been keeping you updated on Shamus' progress. He's out of surgery now. I can get you in to see him, but—"

"No. I want to go…just take me home. If there's anything wrong after…later, when Cain gets home, I'll see that he looks at me. But I want a shower."

She really wanted to crawl into a deep hole and hide out. Lilliane knew that most of the thoughts going on in her head were things that would never normally bother her, but having all this time to think…well, she didn't like herself very much right now. And she was reasonably sure that no one else was happy with her either.

"All right. I'll take you there, but I'm supposed to take you to the emergency room after. I'm not fucking around with Alyssa. She's pissed three ways from Sunday that you were arrested anyway." She was handed the things she'd come in with and signed that she'd received them while Drew continued talking. "Besides, there are things that we need from you about the man you killed. For starters, do you know who he was? Did Shamus tell you anything?"

"Yes, he said the man in the basement worked for Cait. Said he'd been part of my covert. I'm assuming that means that he was sent to watch over me. I never saw him, before you ask. If he was there, it wasn't at any time that I saw him." They stepped outside and she noticed that the sun was still hours from coming up. "The guy on the porch, Shamus said was his partner. I'm not sure what capacity he meant that in, but I'm assuming he meant just in this. The man I killed made a pass at me and told me he was going to have some fun with me." Lilliane shuddered again when she thought about him touching her. She needed a shower right now and hoped that Drew didn't make good on his threat to take her to ER before she could do so. When he turned toward the hospital instead of the house, she growled at him.

"Look, you might have some evidence on you that the cops missed. I need to assure everyone that you're fine. So keep talking and let it go." He handed her a bag and a cup of hot liquid. "I thought you could use some tea and something to eat. There are sugars in the littler bag."

She set about getting the tea sweetened and then opening the bag. Warm, rich smells assaulted her nose. Pastries from the bakery just down the street from her brother's house was her favorite place to eat after she'd come home. She pulled the long cherry and cream cheesed Danish from the bag and moaned when she sank her teeth into the still warm flaky confection. She was half finished when she realized that she should have offered him half. Then she thought, fuck it, he wasn't taking her home. He could suffer.

"The man in the basement, Benjamin Petty, Benny for short, did work for Cait. She said he'd only been working for her just as long as you'd been home. He'd been recommended by another precinct and she should have dug a little deeper before hiring him. She said she'd talk to you later about it." Lilliane nodded. "The man you killed was Art Peck and he and the other man were friends. Both had criminal records, a few small time things, but a great deal of the heavy duty crimes. They'd both spent a good deal of the last ten to twenty in prison."

"Did they know my father?" When he looked over at her briefly, she went on to explain. "Shamus was trying to find a connection to the others through my father. Most of the people who'd committed the attacks on my family were known associates of my father's through prison. He was trying to make a connection."

Drew nodded this time. "I see. No, I don't, but I can see where this is going. As for your father...I don't know. If they were then that would be a whole new set of issues." She started to tell him about the man in the mall, but they were pulling up in front of the hospital emergency doors then.

Lilliane knew they were going to find a few bruises she'd not had before. When they'd been driving over to the house where Shamus had been she'd tried to get away from Art because he'd pulled her body so close to his. He'd grabbed her breast and pinched it. She'd been trying to adjust her bra away from the soreness since she'd been arrested. Since she'd not wanted to bare her boob in an open cell she'd just simply tried to deal with it.

The emergency room wasn't very busy at two in the morning. She'd been expected so they simply rushed her back to one of the empty rooms. Damon Grant showed up a few minutes later with her brother. Cain pulled her into his arms for one of his bear hugs and she nearly passed out from the pain. When he let her go, she must have looked in pain because he lifted her up and sat her on the bed.

"Damn it, Cain, what's wrong with you? I'm quite capable of—"

"Hush. We're going to examine you to make sure—"

"Cain," Damon said softly but with authority, "you're going to step out now while I look your sister over. I'm sure she'll feel much better with you out of the room." Lilliane thought she heard him mumble that he would too, but didn't say anything.

Cain looked ready to argue. But in the end, he turned and walked to the door. He turned back to them both before he left and glared at her, but spoke to Damon. "I want a full report, please. And there will be a full explanation from you on what the fuck you thought you were doing trading places with Sin. And so you know, she's on my shit list too."

Damon waited for a full minute before he sat on the bed beside her. His face was lit with humor. She smiled in return.

"He can be a bit bossy, can't he?" Lilliane nodded. "Can't blame him. You're his sister, after all. I'd do the same for my sisters-in-law. Of course, any of the five of them can kick my ass all over the floor and back, but can't blame a man for trying to protect what he loves."

She looked away from his face when she felt the tears threaten. "I killed that man. In the past several months, I've killed...three people are dead because of me and Shamus is...Shamus is fighting for his life."

"Lilliane, I don't think you believe you had anything to do with those men being dead." She started to say she had when he raised his hand. "Don't get me wrong, you were the instrument that ended their lives, but you in no way had anything to do with their deaths. The moment they picked up a gun to come after you or whoever else, they died. You just were the one that saved the police the trouble."

"And Shamus? You can't tell me that I had nothing to do with him being here. If he hadn't been here then...then he'd be where he really wants to be right now." She wiped at the tears and wondered if she'd ever stop crying. "He's gone through so much because he was supposed to be watching over me."

Damon didn't say anything as he stood up. He pushed the little button on the nurse call switch and asked for someone to come and assist him. He looked at her after he was told someone would be right in.

"Do you think he's not where he wants to be, young lady? I mean, besides the recovery room. You don't think he is right where he wants to be? With you?"

"No. He wants to go back to Tennessee. He has a job there as soon...I guess now. This is over with and now he can go back to his real job." The nurse came in with a small cart of equipment then and prevented her from continuing. But apparently not Damon.

"You're just stupid if you think that." His tone hurt, but she knew better. Shamus had told her and everyone listening to the recording of their conversation that there was nothing between them.

Kathi S. Barton

174

Chapter 20

Shamus woke to the strangest sound. He opened one eye and looked around the room to find the…baby crying?

A woman was sitting in the chair right in front of him holding a screaming kid and seemed to be enjoying herself. He cleared his throat before he spoke and she looked right at him and smiled. He hadn't been able to make out a damned thing because everything was so blurry.

"We were beginning to think you'd never wake up. Here, I have to call the nurse." He still had no clue who the woman was until she spoke again. "It's Alyssa. Cain said you'd be sort of groggy and your vision would be slightly impaired. It's the drug from the surgery. Well, that and the several blows to your hard head."

"Where…" He found that his throat was sore, dry, and his tongue felt like he'd been on a bender for a week or so. "Lilliane all right?"

The nurse came in then and he closed his eyes against the flare of the light when she turned it on. He answered the questions she asked. Did he remember how he'd gotten there? No, but he knew he'd been hurt and kidnapped. Did he remember his name? Yes, Shamus McKee. He must have faded out after that because the next thing he knew he was waking up again.

This time Cain was sitting there when he opened his eye. He figured that the person who'd hit him was the reason he couldn't see but out of one eye at the moment. Cain appeared to be sleeping and Shamus wondered again where Lilliane was.

He had no idea what the date was. He didn't even know what time it was. The room was shadowed in darkness, but that could have been from the heavy drapes that were closed. He could smell the sweet scent of flowers and the sharp smell of hospital, but nothing else. The sounds he could hear were muted, like they'd come through a long tunnel. He wanted to roll over, to look around the room more, but he just didn't have the energy. When he looked back at Cain he was awake.

"How are you feeling? You can't have anything for pain for another hour, but I can rush it a little if you need it." Cain sat up and took his wrist. "You're doing a lot better than you should be, so I'm glad for that."

Shamus wasn't sure how to take that so he didn't say anything back. "Lilliane, where is she?" Cain stood up, went to the drapes, and pulled one corner of them back slightly.

"She's...she's at work." Cain turned back to him and took his seat again. "A lot has happened since you were brought in. They know the name of both the men that took you. Payton and Sin have been working on connecting some of the information you gathered. The house you were in, it was rented by one of the two. It's easy to see the paper trail they laid, Payton said. He was—"

Shamus felt his body seem to relax by degrees. He knew that he should have fought the exhaustion, but his body needed sleep more than he needed information. And he wanted to know where Lilliane was. He vaguely realized that Cain was giving him the runaround.

The next time he opened his eyes, he knew he was stronger. Well, maybe not stronger, but at least more rested. Alyssa was back this time and she had a laptop in front of her and she was doing that thing with her water bottle again. He watched her shake it, squeeze it, and generally treat it as if it was about to explode.

"It's water, not a bomb. Just open it and fucking drink it." She jumped slightly then smiled at him. He realized he'd spoken out loud when he should have kept his mouth shut.

"When I was seventeen my father died. Daddy left everything to me and nothing for the rest of them. He'd found out that my brothers weren't his children and that my brother Nathan was my uncle's, his own brother's child. My mother had been having an affair with him for nearly all their married life." She opened the bottle and took a large drink before continuing. "After the reading of the will, I met my mother and my two brothers with my uncle at a restaurant. They informed me that I was going to have a baby. My uncle's, as a matter of fact. And to accomplish this they drugged my glass of tea. After that, well, I have a few issues with open containers still."

He figured there was much more to the story than she was telling him. But he could see how much of what she'd told him had cost her. She looked not only sad but pissed off as well.

"I'm sorry. I didn't know. And I'm sorry about your dad. I lost mine not long after I got out of high school. He told me the only reason he didn't die sooner was because he'd promised my mom that he'd wait until I was a man." There was more to his story as well, and he thought she knew it.

"Cain said you'd asked him about Lilliane. He didn't tell you, did he?" Shamus started to shake his head then stopped. Pain ricocheted through his entire body. "I thought not. I love him very much, but he was afraid if he told you you'd either not care or…well, he wanted you to get better."

"Where is she? Is she hurt?" His pulse hiked up and he heard the little beeping sound he'd just noticed behind him. The door opened and three people came in with a big cart. Alyssa was moved away and he was suddenly being treated like he'd just been shot...again.

It was over twenty minutes later when he was finally left alone. He looked around for Alyssa and saw that her computer and her briefcase were gone as well. He was getting sick and tired of not getting any answers. But before he could try and figure out where to get his answers, a nurse came in and he was drifting off again. Damn it all to hell was all he thought before he was out again.

Sin was sitting there this time. He knew it was light out because someone had opened the drapes and sunlight was pouring in. It hurt a little, but soon his eye adjusted to the brightness. Sin was smiling at him when he looked at her again.

"When I woke up in the hospital all I wanted anyone to do was to open the fucking curtains. Of course I was on a ship and the windows weren't near this big, but light is light." She stood up and sat on the side of his bed. "Are you going to go all ape shit on me like you did yesterday or will you let me talk to you?"

"Talk. But where is your sister? No one will tell me dick." She laughed at him. "You were a lot more helpful at the house."

She grinned and went back to the chair. "Wasn't me. I know she told you it was, but I was at home with my hubby and daughter."

Shamus tried to think. She'd told him she was Sin. But he'd known. He'd known it was her from the start. He looked over at Sin. Her grin told him she knew a lot more.

"You told her yet?" He didn't even pretend to not understand her. "The reason I ask is because she's under the misconception that you don't. Love her, I mean. But you do, don't you, very much so if your face is any indication."

"Yes, I do. And no, I haven't told her yet. I just figured it out before I was taken. I was going to the school to tell her when that dick head took me." He had a thought. "She killed a man, another man. How is she taking that?"

Sin shifted in her chair and brought her feet up and sat on them. She reminded him of a cat, sleek and not willing to give an inch. "Not too bad, she tells us. But then we don't really know because she's moved. The doctor said you'd be able to leave if you have someone to watch over you at home."

"Moved? Moved where? How could you let her just..." Shamus closed his eye. "She's moved away to get away from me. Christ, I'm a royal screw up. I told her that we were just temporary, that as soon as this was over I was going my way and she hers. I guess she figured she'd go first."

"Humm. Could be. Or then again, it could be that she's waiting for you to come and get her. I don't really think that's what she's doing, but..." Her tone sharpened more. "You hurt her, you ass. I told you not to do that or I'd kill you. You surely didn't believe I was kidding, did you?"

He remembered the "talk" the Waite women had had with him. Mostly it was them telling him not to hurt her or they'd have to answer to him, but Sin had told him that her twin had been hurt by someone once and that she figured she'd never find anyone to love her like she'd wanted. Lilliane had felt her entire life that she was less than a real person and had taken up teaching to have someone look up to her even if it was because of height and not because they thought she was special.

"I don't...didn't think she and I were compatible. I thought because of her money and my lack of it—"

Sin burst out laughing. He didn't think what he was saying warranted her belittling him and nearly told her so. But she spoke first.

"Money? You think she has money? She hardly has a pot to piss in. The money any of us have is because of our spouses. Nathan Howard, have you heard of him?" Shamus nodded. Who didn't know the richest man in the world? "Alyssa is his daughter. And when she and Cain married, she made him sign a pre-nup. It said that all that was hers was his and his was hers. She told him later that if he tried to divorce her, she thought he should just kill himself, it would be less painful. Quinn married into the Miller fortune. Substantial money there as well. Same sort of set up between them as well. My husband's family money is as old as his name. They are the wealthy of old money and he told me that he didn't care if we didn't have anything but each other. So you telling my sister that you weren't good enough for her…well, fuck tard, that just doesn't fly." Sin went to the door. "She's moved and I'm so not going to help you find her. You're on your own. She's been offered a teaching position that starts with the new school year. You have about five weeks to find her and get her to believe in you or I hunt you down."

She left after that and he laid his head back on the bed. Christ, he had fucked up royally again. Shamus reached for the phone and decided that he'd better start now or he'd never find her. He had a feeling that one, if not all, of the Waites would do their damndest to not help him more than they would help right now. He called the only man he knew for certainty would at least give him some help.

"Hello, Peter, it's Shamus McKee. I was wondering what you could do to help me find the woman I love?"

"Hot damn, boy, you surely pissed off them rich people," he said with a hardy laugh. "You tell me what you need and I'm all for helping you. By the way, I've been…put on administrative leave down here. Seems the mayor didn't take too kindly to me telling her what I thought of her mayoral position. You know my motto, don't you?"

"Yeah," Shamus said as he laughed. "Don't ask me if you don't want the answer."

They both laughed for several more minutes as Peter told him what he'd said. "Apparently, it's considered bad form to tell her if she got up off her fucking big ass and helped instead of interfered with a case then our crime rate would drop rather than go up. She used more than eighty thousand dollars of tax payers' money to redo her office last month. Don't think she's going to be up for a reelect. Especially when they just had to lay off nine firefighters and over a dozen cops."

Shamus wondered about the job he'd been promised and realized he really didn't care. He didn't want to move anywhere that he didn't have Lilliane with him. He grinned when he thought of the look on her face when he found her. She was going to be in for a big surprise when he did. Yeah, living life with his little school teacher was going to be fun.

"I need to find Lilliane Waite. I haven't a clue where she is. I'm sure we have enough information on her from the shooting that we could use, don't we?" He thought about what her sister said. "She's just applied for a teaching position somewhere. Will that help?"

Peter laughed. "Yeah, but I'm way ahead of you. Been running a check since you said you needed help finding somebody. She's in Florida. Got a teaching…shit, she's working at one of the worst high schools in that district. Want me to go and get her?"

He wanted her here now, but didn't know what she'd do if he sent Peter after her. He thought maybe Peter would be safer staying away from her for the moment. He thought maybe he would too, but he didn't have much of a choice.

"No. I'll get her my way. I might have to pull some strings and kiss a few asses, but I think I'll handle this my way." He smiled. "She's never going to know what hit her."

Peter was still laughing when he hung up a few minutes later. Shamus closed his eye and tried to think past the pain. He was in pain too, but decided that he wasn't going to take anything more for it. He needed to get up and going and being out in la la land wasn't going to help him get his woman. Slipping into sleep, he thought maybe he was going to see if she'd let him taste her as soon as she got here and decided quickly he might be better off waiting until he could defend himself better first. But he so wanted her beneath him right now.

~~~

Peter arrived the next morning. He had all the information he could obtain about the school she was at, where she'd been staying, and what she'd been up to for the past three weeks. Shamus had been stunned to realize he'd been out for so long.

When his doctor, a Michael Preston, came in a short time later, Shamus asked the doctor how long before he could get up and about. The doctor seemed hesitant to speak in front of Peter, but after he'd showed the doctor his ID without his badge, he sat down.

"You have muscle damage in your leg. The bullet that entered your thigh went into the large muscle, tore up some major muscles, and nicked your artery. Had you not gotten to us when you had, you'd be dead."

Shamus felt his blood run cold. "Will I be able to… Can I walk again?"

"Yes. But I'm afraid your days as a cop are over. I'm sorry, young man. You will be able to get around well. You'll have a limp, but you were able to keep your leg. Like I said, any more time and we might not have been able to save you or your leg either."

Shamus felt…he wasn't sure yet. He did feel something, but what he couldn't tell. Hurt, ashamed, angry, hell, he even felt like he was relieved. But he just couldn't quite nail down what he was feeling most. He looked over at Peter.

"What do I do now?" He looked at the doctor when he cleared his throat. "You got an idea, doc?"

"Yes. I think you should work your ass off and prove me wrong. Giving up…well, I know the Waites. Cain is a good friend and I'm pretty sure that you're going to have a rough time of it if you try and give up. That one sister…I think her name is

Sydney? Well, I'm sure she'll get you into shape if you asked her."

Shamus laughed. The doctor didn't know the half of it. She'd probably put him in his grave if she thought it would protect her sister. He and the doctor spoke some more before he left. Shamus now had another whole set of things to take care of.

Chapter 21

Lilliane sat at her table and put her hand over her belly again. She was so nervous she couldn't think. She was sure that the first thing she was going to do next week when she got to the school was throw up on someone. She wasn't sure she could do this; she was positive she couldn't. She picked up the phone for the tenth time and this time, dialed the number.

An hour later she was in her little cramped bedroom when she heard someone at her door. She hoped it wasn't that paper kid again. She was tired of him coming by daily to talk to her. She didn't want the flipping paper and she didn't want to have to call someone to get him to stay away. She wrenched open the door to blast him once and for all.

"Fuck me." Shamus was there.

"Now is that any way for a teacher to talk? Shame on you." He barged right on in past her. "I hope you know whatever it's cost me to fly down here is coming out of my fees. I don't think you realize how much this thing is costing me."

She closed the door behind him. He was really there. When he reminded her to lock it, she simply turned the lock as if he had a right to be on this side of the door with her. She thought perhaps she was dreaming when he stumbled toward her.

"I'm not very good on these things yet. But I'm getting there." He tossed the crutches to the floor as he got closer to her.

"Of course, had you been where you should have been, I could have gotten better on them slower."

His mouth brushed over hers gently. She wanted more and leaned up to press her mouth against his more firmly. When he took her mouth this time, it was hungry, hot, and oh so delicious. When he pulled away, she whimpered.

"I missed you." His mouth trailed down along her throat as he pressed open mouth kisses around her neck. "I've missed you a great deal."

Suddenly, she realized that he really was here and she pulled away. He wobbled, but seemed to catch himself before he fell. She nearly reached out to him but caught herself. He wasn't supposed to be here.

"You wasted your money. I want you… You need to leave. I've got things to do and places to go. I don't even know why you're here."

"I'm not leaving. I was hired to keep an eye on you until this thing is over or until I thin—"

"It is over, you jackass. Two dead guys make it completely over. And in case you hadn't gotten the memo, you've been cleared by Alyssa to return to work. Now, I want you to leave right now. Like I said, I have things to do." She went to the door and started to open it only to find herself pressed against it.

"You quit your job an hour ago. Which is good, you know. I'd hate to have to sell my part of the partnership I made with your brother-in-law so soon after working out the contract specs on our new business." His mouth was back to doing strange and wonderful things to her throat. She could feel her pussy heating up. When his teeth nipped at her earlobe, she moaned.

"I want you. I want to take you right now against this door, but I'm afraid I'd drop us both." He tugged the zipper of her dress down and followed it with his mouth. "Of course being on the floor with you does sound good too."

His cock rocked into her ass. She couldn't help pressing back into him. His groan made her pussy clench with need. When she tried to turn around he held her in place with his leg between hers.

"You should stop this now. We're…you said that you didn't…that this was—Oh my gosh, Shamus, please." His teeth sank into shoulder and she nearly came right then. "You have to stop this. I don't…I don't want you."

His whispered, "Liar" nearly made her melt. He moved the dress from her shoulder more and it fell to her hand. When he took the other side down, she wanted to turn again. He still held her.

"If you turn around I'm going to fuck you right here. I don't have the strength in my leg just yet to do that so, for now, I'm going to do this until I have you completely naked and begging me to take you."

She thought she was fairly close to that right now. She pressed back against his cock again and he moaned. She wasn't going to last much longer, she knew, and when he cupped her breast beneath her bra, she reached behind her and cupped his cock.

"Shamus, either take me or let me go. I swear that I can't— Oh Christ!"

His finger slid over her pussy. Even through her dress skirt she could feel him fucking her this way. She rode him as he rocked into her from behind. Reaching up to where his arm leaned on the door, she pulled his hand down to her mouth and sucked his finger.

"Mother of…Christ, woman. I wanted to talk to you first. But that's not going to happen." He bit her shoulder again and she laved her tongue over the tip of his finger and nipped him. "Bedroom. Now."

She leaned over to pick up his crutches when he finally released her. When his fingers dug into her hips and he brought her ass to his groin she didn't move away. She sat up slightly and leaned heavily on his crutches still clutched in her hands.

He let her go with one hand as he lifted her dress from her ass. His groan made her remember she'd put on her thong to boost her confidence. The sound of a zipper being moved across its teeth had her turning to see him.

His cock was just being released from his briefs. The cream on the tip made her want to turn and suck it off, but he fisted himself and rubbed it along his shaft. He looked down at her bent over in front of him.

"This is your fault. I meant to be romantic and now all I can think about is fucking you until you can't walk." He stumbled slightly. "We have to get to the couch. I can't…I'm going to hurt me if I do this the way I want."

She stood up and pulled away. They both whimpered at the same time. Lilliane handed him the crutches and led him to the bedroom. Once there, she reached up and started to unbutton his shirt, her fingers clumsy with need. His mouth was busy on hers and she couldn't seem to concentrate on two things at once so she tore it open.

They were both breathing hard. When she touched her fingers to his chest she felt his heat, felt his heart pounding under her fingertips. When she found his nipple she looked up at him as she leaned down and ran her tongue over the pert tip. She felt his groan as it moved up his chest and out of his mouth. He started to walk her back to the bed.

When her legs touched the mattress she stopped and stepped back. She dropped her dress, which had gathered around her waist, to the floor and stepped out of it. Next, she took off her bra. Her breasts felt full, tight, and her nipples thick with need. When she slipped her panties off she sat on the bed and helped him finish pulling his pants off. Then when he was as naked as her, she took his cock into her mouth.

"Christ," Shamus hissed. She only meant to taste him, to bring him and his taste into her mouth. But he tasted too good to stop and when he tangled his fingers into her hair she took her time. All too soon, though, he was pulling her back.

"My cock is very willing to fuck that luscious mouth, but the body isn't. If I don't lay down soon I'm going to fall down. I'm sorry, baby, but I can't stand up much longer."

She scooted to the middle of the bed and lay back. She watched as he dropped the crutches again and lay down beside her. He lay there for several seconds clenching and unclenching his fists and she knew he was in very serious pain.

"If you want, we can talk now. We don't have to have sex." She started to move off the bed.

"If I'm not buried in you within the next five seconds I'm going to come by just thinking about how hot your pussy is and how much I want it over me." He pulled her closer. "Ride me, Lilliane. Straddle me and take me into your heat. I'm begging you."

She leaned down and kissed him and, careful of his leg, she moved over him and spread her pussy over his hard cock. She knew she was soaking him; her juices had been tickling her thighs since he'd touched her. When he moved her hips up and down she sat up and lifted her body off his. While he held his cock upright for her she slowly lowered herself over and on top of him.

Neither of them moved for several seconds. Just the feel of his cock inside of her was nearly enough. When he dug his fingers into her hips again she looked down at him.

He was beautiful. His face was hard in his lust, but he still looked beautiful. She moved tentatively and felt him surge up. When he pulled her forward then back, she rode him in the rhythm he set. Long, slow rolls of her hips, hard thrusts of his hips. When he sat up and pulled her hips closer to him; she nearly cried out when he took her breast deep in his mouth. His fingers digging into her ass made her ride him faster, harder until she knew she was going to come soon. So when he nipped her nipple, she shattered.

She screamed out his name and felt him roll her over. As soon as her back hit the bed, he was pounding into her. Once, twice, then a third time he hit the sweet spot deep within her before she was coming again. This time she felt him stiffen above her before she felt his cum fill her. His roar of release brought her again as he mouth claimed hers.

She knew that he had to hurt. She'd tried to be careful of his leg, but she had bumped it several times. When he rolled to his back, she heard him moan and knew that he was hurting badly.

"Do you think you can find my pain pills?" he asked her after taking several deep breaths. "I left them…I left them in my luggage in the car. I'm sorry, baby, but I hurt bad enough to cry right now."

She got up quickly and reached for her sweatpants she kept on the chair by the bed to sleep in. "I'll need your keys. And where at in your luggage?"

He told her that they were in the front seat in the small shaving kit. She could see the tremors of pain in his leg. His hiss of breaths made her scared and she pulled her tee on without bothering with shoes. She was back in less than five minutes. When she got him a bottle of water and the two pills, she went to the bedroom in time to see him trying to get up.

"Where do you think you're going? Get back in that bed right now." He glared. "I'm not kidding, Shamus. If you don't lie down right now, I'm going to incapacitate you then drug you up."

"If you must know, I have to pee. Shit, woman, you made me forget everything. Give me my crutches so I can take care of this."

She helped him up and, when she offered to help him while he went to the bathroom, he glared at her and shut the door in her face. Lilliane didn't laugh until he was in the closed room. She heard him cussing when the toilet flushed. As soon as the door opened, she was right there beside him.

"Your bathroom is too small for a large man and crutches. We'll have to find a bigger place and soon." She didn't comment on his declaration. When he got back on the bed he was pale and his skin was damp. She handed him the two pills.

"I only take one. Two makes me pass out and I hate the feeling I get when I wake. It's as if I'm thick or something."

She held them both out to him. "Either take them your way or I'll sit on your chest and cram them down your throat and then soak you while I pour water in after them."

He glared, she stared. Finally he took them both from her and put them in his mouth. Before she gave him the water, she asked to see into his mouth.

"You don't trust me? Damn it, give me the water." When she held it back, he finally put the other pill in his mouth he'd palmed then showed her they were both in there. She held the water to his mouth as he drank.

"You should have been a head nurse somewhere, not a teacher. I bet they love it when you pull that General Waite stuff on them."

She helped him lay back and she was covering him up when she answered. "I usually don't have to ask more than once before they see it my way. Next time I tell you to do something, I want—Shamus!"

He'd pulled her back down onto the bed with him. "I want to sleep with you beside me. I hate these pills, but I guess you're right. I do hurt enough for them both."

"See that you remember that I'm right." She lay next to him and rested her head on his shoulder for about twenty minutes. She wanted to wait until after he'd rested, but she needed to know. "Why are you here?"

He yawned and pulled her close to him before he answered. "Because I love you. And I can't live without you."

She lay there for a good ten minutes after he said that. She kept waiting for him to tell her he was kidding. When she sat up to look at him there was a goofy smile on his face that was relaxed now in sleep.

He loved her? No, that couldn't be right. She'd misheard him. Or he was too doped up to realize what he'd said. She lay her head back down and wondered what she'd do if he did indeed love her. Well, she thought, she didn't have a clue.

But one thing she did know. She was glad she'd not taken the teaching position.

Chapter 22

Ginny sat in the destroyed room. There was very little, if anything, that she'd left in one piece. Even the comforter had been shredded and the pillows, down filled, had been torn open and feathers were on everything that had a flat surface.

She'd come here just after she'd read the newspaper article about the botched kidnapping of one Detective Shamus McKee three days ago. There was also a bit about the rescue of him by none other than Lilliane Waite, school teacher and sister-in-law to the richest woman in the world, Alyssa Waite.

Ginny read the small reports in the paper as they came out with something new. It seemed every day there was some other bit of information, some more to the story that they'd release. It was about the bodies being found, the house that had been rented, and of the phones that had been hidden. Then the entire article had come out, all three pages of it. Ginny picked up the book she'd missed tearing up and started ripping pages from it one and at time.

She'd not seen this coming. Not seen Lilliane being strong enough to fight back and to kill someone Ginny had hired. She expected the bitch to cower in the corner, to find her dear McKee dead in the chair and to fall apart. But she'd done none of that. In fact, she'd done everything the exact opposite of what she'd believed. Ginny hated this one more than she did the cunt army brat.

The articles had mentioned Nathan Howard and Roscoe, her Roscoe, and how he'd tried to use his own cunt daughter as a hostage when he'd not gotten what he deserved. It had mentioned how the poor Alyssa Howard had been tangled up in this affair before she married Cain. Ginny wanted to hunt down the person who wrote that Roscoe was "a sick individual who should never have been let out of the prison system" and rip them to shreds.

Then it went on to say how the poor detective had been injured so badly that he had to retire from the force. That because some "maniac" had shot him at point blank, it had ruined his career. Ginny had been thrilled about that. Guinevere had also done a little jig about it. The two of them had laughed for hours.

Ginny looked up into the mirror when she saw Guinevere enter. She didn't move from the floor, but she did stop tearing the book up.

"Are you going to the meeting with Cain or am I?" Ginny asked her. The appointment had been made several days ago, just after the fucking cop had been released from the hospital.

"Me. He won't understand you." Ginny sneered at Guinevere's reflection. "Well, he won't. The last time you talked to him, he was pissed for months."

"I don't understand how you can stand to be in the same room with him and not want to fuck his brains out." Ginny had only said it for shock value, but Guinevere didn't rise to the bait.

"What are we going to do about this mess?" she'd asked her with an emphasis on the we. "It has to be cleaned up soon. Especially if one of them brats drops by."

Ginny shrugged to both. She hated Guinevere's fucking kids and didn't care if the mess ever got cleaned up.

"The best I can tell you is to have your wonderful son get us a maid. I don't do house work. I've told you this a thousand times." Ginny started tearing out the pages again. The sound reminded her of the sound a knife made as it slid under the skin. She looked up when Guinevere spoke again.

"I suppose you have another plan. I think we should lay low for awhile. The paper said they have this new equipment set up and they were getting closer and closer all the time to finding out things."

Ginny tossed the book at the mirror and was disappointed that the glass didn't shatter. "They also said that your wonderfully rich daughter-in-law was giving a fund raiser for the police department in appreciation for all their hard work. What the fuck about my hard work? If it wasn't for me then they wouldn't need the money for her to raise."

Ginny dared Guinevere to try and puzzle that one out. To be honest, it had made a great deal more sense in her head before she said it. But she didn't say anything and went away. Ginny sat in the room.

It was a mess, but she didn't care. The things in the room belonged to the house and not to her or Guinevere. "Its furnished," Cain had told his mother the first time he'd brought her here, and hadn't offered once to have it replaced for them. The stuff laying about the floor, books, magazines, and other smaller stuff had also been "furnished" with the house. Ginny looked down at one of the magazine covers on the floor.

On the cover were Alyssa and Cain. Rage like she'd never felt before surged through her. She picked up the cover, ripped it from the magazine, and tossed the other pages away. She stared at the picture of the two of them and thought of her own face staring back at her, her own arm around Cain's, and the baby...well, the baby simply gone. She looked at the date. Almost three months ago.

Folding the cover up carefully, she tore it along the seam she'd just made. When she was satisfied that it was perfect she tore it along the seam until all she had was a picture of Cain and the arm of the woman that hadn't been her and a leg of the baby. She stood up, walked over the mess, and went to the bed. She was going to have to get herself a frame, she thought, and then put it by her side of the bed. Smiling for the first time in days, Ginny closed her eyes, remembering at the last minute to call out to Guinevere to set the alarm for her appointment with Cain.

~~~

Shamus woke suddenly. He wasn't sure for several seconds where he was, but a hand patting his chest and soft words about being safe had him relax again. He looked down at the sleeping woman on his arm and smiled.

He felt her warmth and adjusted the blanket over them both when she moaned. Her feet moved along his leg and he moaned himself. She snuggled her face into his neck and it was all he could do not to roll her over to her back and take her again. But he did pull her slightly closer.

"You're going to be sore if you keep moving like that. There is another pain pill and a bottle of water on the other side of the bed." Her voice was low and soft, the perfect cadence of someone who was barely awake after sleeping for awhile.

"I don't want another pill. I'm not near as sore as I was." He kissed the top of her head. "I wouldn't mind if you wanted to ride me again. I'd gladly take two pain pills if you want."

She leaned up on her elbow and looked at him. He could make out her face and that fact that she was smiling at him. The room had a soft glow and he realized that a lamp across the room had been turned on, or it had been left on. When they'd entered this room he'd not really noticed much other than her.

"You've been asleep for almost fourteen hours. I bet you're hungry." She started to roll off him when he tightened his arm around her. "What is it? Do you have to go to the bathroom again?"

"No," he told her softly. He was still thinking about the amount of time he'd been asleep. "Have you been here the whole time?"

She snorted. "I have a life, believe it or not. By the way, how did you know that I'd...you've been tracking me." She pulled away again and he let her this time.

"Yes. I won't lie. I've known where you were for almost the entire time. I couldn't...it took me awhile to come to you because of my leg. I wanted to be able to walk to you." He pulled himself up in her bed and leaned against the headboard. "We need to talk about some things."

"No, we don't. You never answered me. Why are you here anyway? I'm sure that Alyssa told you that you're free to go." He nodded. "Then what?"

"I told her it wasn't complete, that the woman was still a missing piece of the puzzle. And until we find her, then the rest of you are in danger." She wanted to smack him. "And besides, you and me, we've got some things to settle between us."

Like what? She wondered, but didn't ask. "There's no reason why you have to hang around. I'm betting with that new crap in that house, anyone could find out...what are you doing?" She started to back up when he reached for his crutches and stood. He was naked, beautifully so. His cock, semi-hard, seemed to harden with every step he took toward her. "Shamus, you need to rest up before you go back. How did you get here anyway?"

"I came on the Waite company jet. And I'm not going anywhere." He kept coming at her. "Does this have anything to do with what I said to you the night I was shot?"

She hit the wall behind her and realized she'd misjudged where the door was. She was at least another four feet from it. When she glanced toward it, thinking how long it would take her to get there, he caged her in with his hands and the crutches dropped.

"Answer me, Lilliane. Does this have anything to do with what I said to you the night I was shot?"

She didn't want to answer him, but knew that he wouldn't quit until she did. "How did you not know who Benedict Arnold was?"

She knew she was only buying time, but if his confused look was any indication she'd gotten herself more than she thought. Then he apparently remembered.

"Payton got it. He was doing a search on more Arnolds in the department before the cavalry showed up." She must have looked confused because he continued. "The man in the basement, Benny, he was a Benedict Arnold, a traitor to his department. By the time I came out of surgery, Cait had three other men, not any that had been working with this issue, but three others that had suspicious things going on in their accounts. Large, unexplained sums of money. She has since had them arrested."

"So you were speaking code. Why?" She looked up at him when he didn't answer. "You didn't think you were going to make it and you were trying to warn them."

He nodded. "Yes. I knew that I was losing blood fast and knew the chances of me surviving were getting lower all the time. I had to let them know in case there were others. While I'm happy to tell you what I was saying to Payton, you still haven't answered me. So I can only assume that you believed me. I was trying to keep you safe."

She looked down at this chest. "Safe from whom? You or the bad guys?"

When he lifted her chin back up he brushed the tear that had just fallen away with his thumb. He kissed her nose and then brushed his mouth over hers. When he ran his tongue along the seam of her mouth she let him in.

He kissed her softly at first, his tongue dueling with hers with smooth, long strokes. When she answered his dance with one of her own, he groaned and pulled her body to his.

"Lilliane, for a very smart woman, you're incredibly stupid." He laughed when she punched him in the chest. "I love you, woman."

"Why?" She hadn't meant to say it out loud, but she was glad that she had in a way. She needed to know why anyone, especially him, would love her.

"Why?" he asked incredulously. "Why? Well, because you're smart and lovely. You have such a way about you that makes me feel so secure one moment and the need to protect you the next. You're brave and bring out the best in people. You're sexy…very incredibly sexy, and oh so sexy."

"You said that…three times. I'm sure I'm not all that—"

His mouth covered hers. And when he pressed his very, very hard cock into her belly she moaned. Need for him, for this man, only rippled around her skin like a silken caress. He cupped her ass and brought her closer to him as he rocked into her.

"I want you. Come back to bed and let me show you just how much." He wiggled his brows at her and she burst out laughing. "But first, I need to ask you something. Well, I need to tell you something then ask you."

They went back to the bed and he sat down and took several deep breaths before he laid back. She hadn't realized how much he had to be hurting by standing there. She looked down at his leg.

"It's getting better," he told her. "All the time, it's getting better. But I had to come and see you before you started school or your sister was going to kick my ass."

"Sin? What did…I wasn't even aware she knew where I was." She'd not called any of them after she left one afternoon.

She had wanted to think and all she'd managed to do was brood. "How did she find me?"

He reached up and fingered the earrings they had exchanged the day she'd traded clothes with her. Lilliane closed her eyes and remembered her sister insisting that someone would notice her not wearing the type of earrings that she did.

"They're bugged. She said to tell you she's not the least bit sorry either. I guess your sister isn't just a consultant for that firm she works for either. She seemed to think you might try something like this."

"Oh, she'll be sorry all right. Just as soon as I get back to Ohio, she's going to be really sorry." She looked at him when he whooped. "What?"

"Nothing. Your brother-in-law offered me a job. Payton is quitting the force as of next month and we're going to open an investigative office. Cooperider and McKee Investigations will be doing corporate background checks as well as other things on the corporate level. We already have our first client."

"Alyssa." He nodded. "She would make a hard boss but a fair one."

"Yes. The only thing we need is a secretary. You wouldn't know anyone who could answer the phone in a very sexy voice, take dictation, and be bent across my desk when I need her to be, would you?" He wiggled his brows again. "My desk only, by the way."

"Of course. There's Sally Dermott that lives just down the road from Cain, then there is Allison Sheppard that…no, I think she's—"

She found herself on her back and him over her. "You, damn it. I want you. Forever. Lilliane Iris Waite, will you marry me?"

Chapter 23

Guinevere watched them gather at the church. Stupid girl getting married to her gimpy lover was beyond stupid. But what did she really care? Once they were all gone, she'd have what she wanted and it wasn't going to be some lame ass like the cop.

What really pissed her off was the house. Why the fuck was he getting the house? Because he got hurt. She knew what had been said, but there was no way that he of all people should be living in Cain's old house because they felt bad.

Guinevere had told Ginny just yesterday about the house. Also how he'd happened to own it and the small cottage on the property, as well as some kind of equipment that the whore had purchased too. Ginny had had plenty to say about that.

"What do you mean he gets the house in some kind of settlement? Are you telling me because I shot him in the fucking leg he gets the house that we should be living in? Oh, that is so fucked up. You tell Cain we want that house."

Guinevere had started to move back from her anger, but didn't when she saw the look from the reflection in the mirror. "He said that the cop could sue them for what happened and this was going to work out for everyone. He and Lilly Pad would have a house and they'd have a place to work from. His injury put him out of work, you know?"

"I know. I fucking did it. And he should have died, but that fucking cunt of a daughter of yours just had to save his ass. I bet he hates her for that, doesn't he?" Ginny was nodding when Guinevere was shaking her head. "What else are you not telling me?"

"They're getting married. Next week, they're getting married and all of them will be there. I have to…I have to be there too."

The brush hit the wall with enough force to embed it into the plaster. Then came the small perfume bottle; this shattered and spilled its contents everywhere. When Ginny's anger was this bad, Guinevere wanted to hide away from it and let her have her tantrum, but this time she was stuck and had to let it boil out. Things hit the wall across from them and with more and more force. She'd never seen Ginny be that pissed before.

Guinevere was startled from her memories when someone touched her shoulder. It was that ass, the attorney. She hated this man almost as much as she did the daughters. He was telling her that she needed to be seated so he could go back with Shamus and the others.

"I thought I was giving her away with Cain. I asked him and he said he'd ask Lilliane." She didn't really want to, but she had to make people believe she was a happy mother, Ginny had told her. Make nice with the money, she'd said.

"Lilliane wanted just Cain. Now come on, let's get you seated. I told you, I have to get to the back with Shamus and the others." Guinevere wanted to argue with him, go and find Lilliane, and demand that she let her have her way, but the door had been locked to the room where she was getting dressed. The whore, no doubt.

When she was seated she felt Ginny stir. Now wouldn't be a good time for her to appear. It might be fun, but not good. Guinevere spoke softly to her after making sure there wasn't anyone around to hear.

"We're at the church. You said you would behave. You told me that you'd not do anything stupid that would bring attention to us."

Guinevere nodded to a couple behind her when they asked her if she was all right. Or course she wasn't all right. She wanted to scream at them. Her Roscoe was dead and the people responsible were having a grand old time with her money.

"I just wanted to tell you that we really should have done something today. Too bad we didn't have more time to plan. This whole church going up could have taken them all out in one big explosion. Including the brats they spawn like rabbits."

Just why Guinevere didn't tell her until she had. The woman had a temper that was beyond Roscoe's. He would have blown the church too. With her in it, no doubt. Although that would have fucked with Ginny too. Guinevere smiled.

The wedding march started and she watched as the rest of the church stood. She continued sitting. She did look up at her daughters, all in the beautiful dresses that she'd not been a part of picking out. Then over at the men. So many of them standing in their black tuxes. Ginny stirred again but didn't speak. As Cain gave Lilliane to Shamus Guinevere still sat. She knew it was petty, but she was beyond carrying. She supposed that she really didn't have anyone to blame but herself that she'd been locked out of the wedding plans. She'd only been trying to help her daughter make the right choice when she told her again she was marrying the gimp night before last.

"What do you think he's going to do for you when you need him? Did you ever think of that? You'll be the one working for the rest of your life while he sits on his ass getting fatter every day."

Lilliane stiffened a little, but like a good girl she didn't lose her temper with her mother. "He has a job. I told you. He and Payton are going into business together. And we have the house from Alyssa and Cain. We're going to be fine."

Guinevere snorted. "House. You think a house is going to keep you warm? Don't do this, Lilliane. I'm your mother and I...I forbid you to marry this...this half man. You'll go back to teaching and you'll do as I tell you."

Guinevere was satisfied that Lilliane was just coward enough to do as she told her. This daughter had always been the one to do as she was told, unlike Sydney or even that stupid one Gracie. Guinevere was shocked when Lilliane stood up and started pacing.

"I'm going to marry him, Mother. And I would appreciate it if you would stop calling him names. He's the man I love and the man I plan to have children w—"

"Oh Christ, you're not pregnant, are you? Oh Lilliane, get rid of it. There's no telling what sort of defects it will have with him as its sire. I know a good doctor that will abort it for less than—"

"I'm not pregnant. Not yet any way." Lilliane sat down and stared at her. "You really are something, aren't you? You really hate us all so much that... Have you ever loved any of us?"

"Don't be ridiculous. Roscoe wanted children and I, as a good wife, provided them for him. He had good strong morals and he thought he'd breed good children with them. Neither of us dreamed that we'd spawn such ungrateful brats. You'll just do as I say and tell that person you've changed your mind. You'll keep the house, though. And I'll move in with you and things will be better. You'll see I'm right as soon as this entire mess is settled."

Guinevere reached out to take her daughter's hand and was surprised when she snatched it back. She started to tell her to behave when Lilliane suddenly stood up and walked toward the door. Guinevere stood as well.

"You'll come back here, young lady. We've not settled this and you damn well know it." When she opened the door Guinevere said her name sharply. Lilliane finally turned back.

"You'll come to the wedding or not, I could care less, but you'll not be welcome in our home. You'll not be a part of my life, my children's lives, nor that of their children if I can help it. You stay away from me. I mean it, you come near me or mine and I'll hurt you."

With that, she left the house and didn't look back. Ginny made her appearance then. And Guinevere growled at her.

"Hey, I didn't have anything to do with that shit. You did that all on your own. I told you to play nicely with her, not tell her what you really thought."

"She's going to marry that man and I won't have it. I won't have her treat me as if I'm some sort of dirty laundry she's throwing out to the trash heap." Guinevere looked up when Ginny laughed. "You would do well to remember why you're here too."

Ginny's attack was brutal and quick. The pain in her head felt as though a large knife was slicing into her skull and twisting around. Blood poured from her nose until she was sure she would bleed to death. Her muscles in her legs felt like they were being twisted around until they'd snap. Guinevere screamed out as her back bent back. Her fingers began to twist. Then as suddenly as it started, it stopped. Breathing hard and crumpled on the floor, she felt Ginny move.

"And you'll do well to remember who the strong one is."

~~~

The plane landed in Italy at four in the morning the morning after the wedding. The chateau that Alyssa and Cain owned was theirs for an entire week. A week of nothing but making love and having fun until they dropped. Lilliane looked over at her new husband and smiled. "You're beautiful, have I told you that today? Simply beautiful." She blushed at his words. "And I love you."

"Hummm, I love you as well. Very much." She slipped into his arms and hugged him to her. "I'm so glad you talked me into marrying you."

His bark of laughter made her look up at him. She frowned at his look only to have him kiss her quickly on the mouth. "I didn't talk you into anything. If memory serves, you told me that I should have asked you sooner. And you berated me for not having a ring when I asked you."

"I did not berate you. I simply told you that when you ask a woman to marry you it is customary to have a ring. And as for asking me sooner, I most certainly did no such thing. I wasn't even sure that I liked you then."

He kissed her again. This time with more heat. He started backing them toward the bedroom and when they got to the doorway, he stopped and pulled her blouse up and over her head. The rest of her clothes were peeled off as they made it to the bed. She stood before him in just her panties and bra that Gracie had made for her and the dress that she'd designed for her. Lilliane was so glad the crutches were gone.

He started to take off his own shirt when she stopped him. "I want to do it. I want to take you to your skin."

The jacket was easy to take off him. She only had to walk behind him and pull it down off his shoulders and let it fall from his arms. She tossed it to the chair in the corner. When she walked around to his front, she put her hands on his chest and felt his heart pound under her fingers.

"You're so hard. I love the way your muscles feel under my fingertips. The way they ripple." She started at the top of his shirt and slowly worked the button through the tiny hole. "I love the way you smell, manly and warm."

"Lilliane, honey, you're killing me here. Please hurry." He lifted her chin up and kissed her, his tongue twirling along hers in a dance of sensual heat. She pulled back slowly and nipped at his lower lip as she stepped back.

"This is my honeymoon and I want to take you to the stars and back. Please let me do this for you, for us." He nodded. "I love you very much, Mr. Shamus McKee."

"I love you very much, Lilliane McKee."

She resumed with his buttons. When she got the third open, she pressed her mouth to his chest. His breath swooshed from his mouth and she felt it across her hair. The next two buttons were hard for her; she couldn't make them work and finally she just tore them from the shirt. His laugh made her grin.

"They were keeping me from my goal." He pulled her to him again and she felt his cock, its hardness made her pussy weep. "Stop that, you're making me wet."

He groaned and rocked against her again. "You're making me hard. And my cock is so ready to be deep inside of your wetness."

She hurried through taking his shirt off and moved to the belt. He wasn't helping her concentrate by leaning down and taking her nipple into his mouth. When he bit her gently, she slid her hand down the front of his pants and wrapped her hand around his cock and stroked him.

"Lilliane, baby, please," he moaned against her breast. "I need you."

She didn't let him go as she dropped before him. She wanted to taste him, to feel him deep in her throat, coming until he filled her. She pulled his pants down to his thighs and looked up at him.

"I want you to come in my mouth. I want you to come while I suckle at your cock. Will you, Shamus? Will you come for me?"

He didn't answer her, but laced his fingers deep in her hair and pulled her to him. She licked the tip of his cock, her tongue played with the tiny hole as it leaked creamy fluid out. Lapping at him, she moaned when the taste of him settled on her tongue.

"Lilliane," he groaned. He pumped into her mouth gently, his cock filling it completely. She'd taken him before, had him in her mouth, but he'd never come there, never let her taste him the way he had her.

Reaching up, she cupped his balls in her hand and felt them tighten beneath her fingers. When she rolled the heavy sack in her hand, he moaned again and surged deeper into her, touching the back of her throat now. The harder she sucked, the more he rocked, deeper and deeper still. When she wrapped her hand around the thickness of him that she couldn't take in, he tightened his grip on her hair and slammed deep.

"Christ, baby, I'm coming." The first splash of his cum gagged her. She swallowed hard, his cock head slipping down past the tight muscle in her throat, and she moaned. He wasn't being gentle now, but punched her hard with each thrust. She was going to come from just him coming in her mouth. When he suddenly stopped, she whimpered.

"Bed. Now. And I can't...Christ, you're going to get royally fucked." Lilliane hurried to the bed. Before she could get on it he wrapped his arm around her waist and pushed her head down toward the mattress. His cock, still hard, nestled between her legs.

His cock slammed into her quick. She barely had time to brace herself on the bed when he moved again. Her body, primed for a climax, shattered her. She screamed out his name as he roared his own release, his body pouring into hers. She collapsed on the bed with him over her, his weight pinning her beneath him.

The last few weeks had worn her out and as sleep claimed her, she smiled thinking this was the best relaxant she'd ever had.

Chapter 24

"There's a connection here that we're just not seeing. I know there is. All these 'accidents' have been orchestrated by one person. We just have to figure out who." Shamus looked up at the board as he spoke. "There's a string here. I can almost see it."

He wasn't really talking to anyone in particular. Which was good, he supposed. When he turned and looked at the room behind him, everyone was asleep. He looked over at the clock on the wall. Well shit, it was eight-thirty. And that in and of itself wouldn't be so bad if he didn't know they'd started this yesterday at seven, over twenty-four hours ago. He sat in his chair and looked at the wedding picture on his desk. He couldn't believe they'd been back from their honeymoon for almost a month.

They were all there. He and his new wife Lilliane; Cain and Alyssa holding Connor; Drew and Quinn, her with the two boys, Thomas the sixth and James, and Drew holding his daughter, Abida Rose; Sin and Payton holding their little girl, Tonya, and Gracie and Jazzie standing side by side smiling as large as the rest of the clan. He picked up the picture and rubbed his finger over Lilliane's cheek. He had to find out what was going on.

"You know, you could just come home with me and you can do that to me." He looked up at Lilliane when she spoke from the doorway.

"Come here. I need to hold you." She walked across the room and he thought of liquid sex.

She sat on his lap. He turned the chair away from the board, but she turned them back with a frown on her face. She got up and walked to the pictures they'd just gotten in. They were pictures of the two men, Peck and Petty, and the woman they thought was in charge.

The men had kept notes on where to meet this person. They never mentioned her name, only called her "boss" when they made marks on the calendar they had in the house he'd been held in. And after going back over surveillance cameras in the different meeting places, they'd gotten a few stills of this mystery woman. But so far all they had was the back of her head and a few very blurred pictures of her face.

"Do you know who that is, baby?" She nodded then shook her head. He didn't say anything. He knew what it was like to have a memory tug at you but you couldn't catch it.

"I think I might, but I can't…it's almost as if I should know her." She turned to him. "Do you? Know her, I mean?"

He shook his head. "No. We can't get anything on her other than what you see there. There are some dates they meet with her and a few videos of her with them. But she's either very smart or extremely lucky. I'm thinking its luck."

Lilliane looked at the pictures of the men, all of them that they'd hung up on another board. All the men that had anything to do with any of the recent accidents, including the ones to her. She fingered the one of her father but said nothing. She walked to yet another board and stared at it.

Here were pictures of the family. Each person had a small bio of what had happened and those involved. She turned to him when she'd studied it for awhile.

"This one, you think that it all started with Quinn and my father, don't you?" She didn't ask so much as make it a statement so he didn't answer. "The men with my father and the men with the school, were they related in some way?"

"In a vague sort of way. They knew of your father through a mutual connection. One of their brothers, Peck's, was a floor mate to your father when he'd been in prison. But from what we've been able to find out, they never really knew each other." Shamus looked at the board before he continued. "Petty was a big time player and his release had been a mistake. He'd been in for life because of a murder. How he got out is still being investigated."

She walked back to the wall where the pictures were of the recent men and the woman. "It's the way she's standing. See?" She pointed to the way the woman's hand rested on her hip. "She is standing this way in all of pictures."

Shamus got up and looked. She was right; the woman was stiff, pissed-looking in the stiffness of her shoulders and her stance. He remembered seeing the videos. She'd been waving her arms about and gesturing all over the place. Another memory tugged; this one made a connection.

"Your mother does that. When she's mad, she...she stands like this. I saw her do it at the reception when you wouldn't let her kiss you goodbye."

He hadn't meant to say it out loud, hadn't even realized he'd thought that until she turned to him with a look of horror on her face. Before he could apologize, she was nodding at him.

"I'm not sure...you may think this is weird, but it's not her but it is. Understand? My mother, she would be someone who followed but not anyone who would lead. She'd been..." She looked up at him again. "My mother would go along with anything my father told her to, but this... Could she try and kill her own children?"

Shamus didn't know. He knew there were plenty of strange and crazy people out there, but murder adult children? He wasn't sure. They both turned to Payton when he spoke.

"She's not capable of it. I don't think so anyway. She doesn't have the money for one thing. Cain said she is constantly asking him for money and for another... Well, I'm not sure she's intelligent enough to carry on something this complicated. I agree with Lilliane, if she's involved, and I'm not saying she is, then she's a pawn, not the killer. I think, buddy, that we're barking up the wrong tree there."

"But you said before that women don't do this sort of crime, serial crimes. Could she be the front for another person? A man, perhaps?" Lilliane looked ready to believe it, not that he blamed her. "I mean, what sort of woman kills her own children, adult children? And for what gain?"

Shamus didn't know, but like Payton, he wasn't sure that Guinevere had the brains to be the boss. He pulled Lilliane into his arms as he spoke. "We're all very tired. I think we need to get some sleep and come at this with fresh eyes. Tomorrow we'll come back and look." He turned Lilliane into his arms and looked at her face. "And you, young lady, have to go to work. There are phone calls to answer and dictation to take."

He sent her off with a swat on her ass and smiled when she frowned at him. He was going to have her across his desk before the first phone call came in if it was the last thing he did. He turned to look at Payton when she left.

"What do you really think?" he asked his friend and partner. "You think Guinevere had her children targeted for murder, or is there something we're missing?"

Payton stretched as he stood, his Glock at his hip peeking out from under his shirt. Shamus had been carrying his all the time as well now. He remembered he had a lesson with the other men of the family today and tomorrow to go over the basics of gun handling. He wondered if they would ever feel safe again.

"I think you're right on all levels. But before I answer, I want coffee, food, and my wife." He grinned. "By the way, she's pissed at you."

"Me? What the hell did I do?" He was actually kind of afraid of Sin Cooperider. She could take him out with a single punch. She had been the one who'd taught his own wife how to kill a man.

"She said you're a sexist bastard and she is going to teach the women how to defend themselves and then challenge you all to a death match." Payton laughed. "But I'm exempt."

Shamus was almost afraid to ask why, but he did anyway. He was glad his wife was gone; he hated to give her more ammunition to tease him about. The blush he was supporting was hot and embarrassing to say the least.

"She said that I have a large cock and she can't live without it. Maybe you should go and prove yourself manly to your own wife so we can both live to see out grandkids."

Shamus decided to do just that.

About the Author

I woke up one morning and decided to give play time to the people in my head who were keeping me awake. Little did I know that they would be so relentless and want their time right now! I wrote for the pure joy of it and to entertain my family and friends. But mostly it was to get more than an hour of sleep without a story playing out. Of course, the more I write, the more they want. So…well, as a result of sleepless days (I work through the night as a gun toting grandma – nope not a vigilantly but an armed security guard) I have lots of stories written.

Hello! My name is Kathi Barton and I'm an author. I have been married to my very best friend Sonny for at times seems several lifetimes – in a good way, honey. And together we have three wonderful children and then the ones we brought into the world - Paul and Dale Barton, Jason and Wendy Barton and Danielle and Ben Conklin. They have given us seven of the greatest treasures on Earth. They don't live at home seven days a week! No, seriously, seven grandchildren – Gavin, Spring, Ben, Trinity, Sarah, Kelly and Kian.